Praise for Jonathan Lethem's

Lucky Alan

"Rich and darkly comic. . . . Astutely cunning social and political satires sit alongside experimental flights of absurdist fantasy and parable, with traces of Lethem's unique slant on magical realism sprinkled in as well. Comparisons might be drawn to writers ranging from Jorge Luis Borges and Haruki Murakami to Margaret Atwood and J. D. Salinger. All of Lethem's stories are enlivened by his wit and provocative wordplay."
—*Chicago Tribune*

"A nimble and resourceful writer."
—*The New York Times*

"Nearly every sentence captures Lethem's sharp wit and copious imagination, reminding us that Lethem himself is perhaps the king of sentences after all."
—*Publishers Weekly*

"Reality-bending fables from the master. . . . Weird, charming, playful, *Lucky Alan* is great fun."
—*The Guardian* (London)

"Taut, darkly funny. . . . [*Lucky Alan*] excels at creating these moments of absurdity that exist not merely for their own sake, but on some level to expose our own tendency to accept the unacceptable, to live hypocritically, and to assuage our guilt with comforting words and superficialities rather than meaningful action."
—*The Huffington Post*

"Lethem's words execute graceful turns and explosive leaps to whatever tempo he sets. . . . Rewards await the reader who commits to this slim volume. . . . *Lucky Alan* is a beguiling addition to a shelf full of uniquely inventive books by a master of genres."
—*Miami Herald*

"A wild ride across the boundaries of language, artifice and genre. . . . This is the joy of reading Jonathan Lethem: you never know what you're going to get. . . . You might guess that Alan's luck runs out, but you'll never guess quite how: Lethem is always one step ahead."
—*Financial Times*

Jonathan Lethem

Lucky Alan

Jonathan Lethem is the *New York Times* bestselling author of nine novels, including *Dissident Gardens*, *Chronic City*, *The Fortress of Solitude*, and *Motherless Brooklyn*, and of the essay collection *The Ecstasy of Influence*, which was a National Book Critics Circle Award finalist. Lethem is a recipient of the MacArthur Fellowship and winner of the National Book Critics Circle Award for Fiction. His work has appeared in *The New Yorker*, *Harper's*, *Rolling Stone*, *Esquire*, and *The New York Times*, among other publications.

www.jonathanlethem.com

Also by Jonathan Lethem

Novels
Gun, with Occasional Music (1994)
Amnesia Moon (1995)
As She Climbed Across the Table (1997)
Girl in Landscape (1998)
Motherless Brooklyn (1999)
The Fortress of Solitude (2003)
You Don't Love Me Yet (2007)
Chronic City (2009)
Dissident Gardens (2013)

Novellas
The Shape We're In (2001)

Story Collections
The Wall of the Sky, the Wall of the Eye (1996)
Kafka Americana (with Carter Scholz, 1999)
Men and Cartoons (2004)

Nonfiction
The Disappointment Artist (2005)
*Believeniks! 2005: The Year We Wrote a Book About
    the Mets* (with Christopher Sorrentino, 2006)
They Live (2010)
Crazy Friend: On Philip K. Dick (2011, Italy only)
The Ecstasy of Influence: Nonfictions, Etc. (2011)
Fear of Music (2012)

As Editor
The Vintage Book of Amnesia (2000)
The Year's Best Music Writing (2002)
The Novels of Philip K. Dick (Library of
    America, 3 vols., 2007–2010)
The Exegesis of Philip K. Dick (with Pamela Jackson, 2011)
Selected Stories of Robert Sheckley (with
    Alex Abramovitch, 2012)

Lucky Alan

Lucky Alan

and Other Stories

Jonathan Lethem

Vintage Contemporaries
Vintage Books
A Division of Penguin Random House LLC
New York

FIRST VINTAGE CONTEMPORARIES EDITION, FEBRUARY 2016

The following stories appeared, in slightly different form, in the following
places: "Lucky Alan," "The King of Sentences," "Procedure in Plain Air,"
"The Porn Critic," and "Pending Vegan" in *The New Yorker*; "Traveler
Home" in Walter Martin and Paloma Muñoz's *Travelers*; "Their Back
Pages" in *Conjunctions*; "The Empty Room" in *The Paris Review*; and
"The Dreaming Jaw, The Salivating Ear" in *Harper's*.

The Library of Congress has cataloged the Doubleday edition as follows:
Lethem, Jonathan.
[Short stories. Selections]
Lucky Alan and Other Stories / Jonathan Lethem. — First edition.
pages ; cm
I. Lethem, Jonathan. Lucky Alan.   II. Title.
PS3562.E8544 A6 2015   813'.54—dc23   2014022146

Vintage Books Trade Paperback ISBN: 978-1-101-87366-3
eBook ISBN: 978-0-385-53982-1

Book design by Michael Collica

www.vintagebooks.com

Printed in the United States of America
10 9 8 7 6 5 4 3 2 1

For Desmond Brown

Contents

Lucky Alan

Lucky Alan

In the months after I'd auditioned for him, I would run into the legendary theater director Sigismund Blondy at the movies, near-empty Thursday matinees of indifferent first-run films—*North Country, Wedding Crashers*—in the decaying venues of the Upper East Side, where we both lived: the Crown, the Clearview, the Gemini; big rooms chopped into asymmetric halves or quartered through the balcony. Blondy saw a movie every afternoon, he said, and could provide scrupulous evaluations of any title you'd ever think to mention—largely dismissals, though I do recall his solemn approval of *A Sound of Thunder,* a time-travel film with a Ben Kings-

ley performance he'd liked. I'd see Blondy when the lights
came up—alone, red scarf and pale elegant coat unfurled
on the seat beside him, long legs crossed—unashamed,
already hailing me if he spotted me first. Blondy dressed
in dun and pastel colors, wore corduroys or a dancer's
Indian pants; in winter he had holes in his knitted gloves,
in summer a cheesy Panama hat. He towered, moved
softly and suddenly, usually vanished at any risk of being
introduced. Soon I'd scan for Blondy whenever I entered a
theater, alone or not. Often enough I'd find him. We never
sat together.

If this multiplex-haunting practice didn't square with
Blondy's reputation as the venerated maestro of a certain
form of miniaturist spectacle (*Krapp's Last Tape* in the
elevator of a prewar office building, which moved up and
down throughout the performance, with Blondy himself
as Krapp, for cramped audiences of five or six at a time),
it didn't matter, since that reputation hardly thrived. I'd
auditioned—talked with him, really—for a role in a
repertory production of several of Kenneth Koch's *One
Thousand Avant-Garde Plays*. Dianne Wiest sat with us
in the back room of the SoHo Italian restaurant in which
the Koch cycle was to be staged, and where this evalu-
ative tête-à-tête took place. She followed our conversation soberly, her unexplained presence typical of Blondy's
Zelig-like infiltration of the city's culture. Within weeks
I'd learned that Blondy'd had a falling-out with the restaurant's proprietor, stranding the enterprise. I'd waited,
expecting some revival of the project, for months. Eventu-

ally I assumed I'd been replaced and kept half an eye on the *Times* for a notice of the thing. But the Koch never surfaced, nor did anything else. Maybe Blondy's run was over. Or on hiatus in some deep ruminative lag. And then, in the months that followed, he gradually became my moviegoing doppelgänger.

The ritual was made official the first time he invited me out for a glass of red after the movie, as though that were the real point of the afternoon. We'd sit at some Madison or Second Avenue wine bar in the dimming hours, invariably alongside those waiting for their dinner dates, those who made even me feel old. Whether Blondy ever felt old I couldn't guess. His grandiosity, his U-turn anecdotes, his contempt for the obvious statement didn't invite such guesses, only the tribute of gratified awe. I gave it. Blondy was like a skater up his own river, a frozen ribbon the rest of us might have glimpsed through trees, from within a rink where we circled to tinny music. The first time we left a movie theater together, before even finishing a glass, I told him I had quit acting. Blondy's intimate smile seemed to say, not unsympathetically, that it was all for the best. We rarely talked about the film we'd just seen; instead we discussed great works—the Rothko retrospective, Fassbinder's *Berlin Alexanderplatz,* Durrell's *Alexandria Quartet,* whatever formed his present obsession. After two or three glasses on an empty belly had made me dizzy—Blondy never showed any effects—we'd part on the sidewalk.

By the time it occurred to me that I hadn't seen Sigis-

mund Blondy in a while, I couldn't have said how long
a while was. Four months? Eight? It seemed to me he'd
been in holey-gloves-and-red-scarf mode the last time
we'd slipped from a theater to a bar, but that didn't
narrow it down much. We were headed back to scarf
weather now. Maybe Blondy had summered somewhere—
Provincetown?—and decided not to return, enlisting
some local company to mount spectacles in a dockwork-
ers bar or a bowling alley's lounge. Sig Blondy, big fish in
a small pond? I knew no more consummate New Yorker,
so I started to worry.

Neither of the two people whom Blondy and I knew
in common had any reason to know that the director and
I spent afternoons together, but when I called—the first
didn't have Blondy's phone number, and the second had
one that he thought was the "old number," then found
another he recommended I try—neither was interested
enough to ask why I wanted to track him down. Perhaps these days Blondy was less well remembered than
I'd assumed. Blondy, likely in his early sixties, always
seemed to me terrifyingly vital, but those in their early
sixties might suddenly fail. Had I entered, without notic-
ing, some quiet bargain struck among the proud bach-
elors of Manhattan to get one another's backs? In my
rapidly evolving fantasy, Blondy became pitiable, myself
a rescuer. I rang the number. Blondy's machine was set to
pick up on the first ring. It figured he'd be an old-school
screener.

"Grahame," he said, interrupting my message. His

tone was munificent, as if congratulating me for having the name I did.

I'd been reaching for words to distill my concern but now scrambled, defensively, for a joke. His relish at having lifted the receiver in the thick of my fumbling seemed akin to his pleasure at our old, ambiguous encounters in theater lobbies, before we'd begun drinking. What I said now was "Don't you go to the flicks anymore, or are you ashamed to take the senior discount?"

"Oh, I go. Every afternoon. Just not in the old *neigh-bore-hood*."

"I miss you," I blurted.

He explained that he'd moved downtown, to Minetta Street. Hiding in plain sight, he called it. He'd spoken in the past of his devotion to the block of Seventy-eighth Street, where for decades he'd held down a rent-stabilized bargain, and of his persistent enchantment with the tribes of dog-walkers and nannies he'd mingled with there, once calling the Upper East Side "the last of the true Manhattan." But I didn't get a chance to ask him why he'd abandoned it. "I've got some questions I want to ask you," he said. "When can you get here?"

"Questions?"

"Better than questions, a *questionnaire*. You'll see."

"You want me to come to Minetta Street? Today?"

"Look, Film Forum is doing Mizoguchi—*Ugetsu*. Ever seen it?" There was something of the director in his bullying and beguiling, but it was in my nature, I suppose, to be directed.

*

Ugetsu astonished me. Discussing it after the two-fifteen matinee, while we looked on Sixth Avenue for a restaurant with a suitable bar, Blondy said that for years he'd felt that two scenes toward the end of the film were reversed from their ideal order—the only flaw, he'd always thought, in a perfect work of art—but that today, sitting at Film Forum, waiting for it, he couldn't spot the flaw he'd earlier been so certain of. "What's pathetic is that I'd presumed to go around all these years sure I knew better than Mizoguchi! It's as though I had to defend myself against the film's perfection." I was awed, as I maybe was supposed to be, at the scrupulousness with which he dwelled on what he cared for. Perhaps I was also awed at the change in our friendship. We'd gone to a movie that Blondy cared about, instead of trash, and for once we'd sat together in the theater, so I could smell Blondy's faint but unmistakable doggish odor. It felt as though I'd stepped into Blondy's script, was now simultaneously the featured performer and the sole audience for the most infinitesimal of his productions.

When we'd settled down with two glasses of Syrah, Blondy drew from his pocket several worn photocopies. "Okay, these are the questions I've been wanting to ask you," he said, as if he'd been expecting my call in the first place.

"Okay."

"They're from Max Frisch's *Sketchbook 1966–1971*. Ready?"

"Sure."

"We won't do the whole questionnaire. I'll pick and choose."

"Sure, fine."

"Are you sure you are really interested in the preservation of the human race once you and all the people you know are no longer alive?"

"Sorry?"

"That's the first question." He resumed his insinuating theatrical murmur. *"Are you sure you are really interested . . ."*

I did my best with the question, told Blondy I thought anyone ought to feel a value in the continuity of the species, but he interrupted. "No, you," he said. "How do *you* feel?"

"Yes, I'd be sad if there were no people."

He leaped to the next question. *"Whom would you rather never have met?"*

My only brush with Harold Pinter had been fiercely disappointing. I began to describe it. Blondy rushed me again.

"Would you like to have perfect memory? Just answer the questions that interest you, Grahame. *If you had the power to put into effect things you consider right, would you do so against the wishes of the majority?"*

"Look, Sigismund, what is this?"

"Are you convinced by your own self-criticism?"

"Too much, I'm afraid."

"Are you conscious of being in the wrong in relation to

some other person (who need not necessarily be aware of it)? If so, does this make you hate yourself—or the other person?"

His voice was so entrancing that I suspected we were both entranced. He might as well have asked to read me poetry, for all that I was persuaded he wanted my replies. I said, "What about *you*, Sig? You answer this one."

He nodded, raised his glass. "And hate myself for it."

Again, I wondered if I heard the sound of a trap snapping shut. Had I delivered my designated line? Were we perhaps getting to the point?

"Who?" I asked.

"Alan Zwelish," Blondy said.

*

Sigismund Blondy had known Alan Zwelish for several years, in the way of a Manhattan neighbor, repeatedly sighting a compelling face in passing instants as one or the other swerved from the street into the entrances of their buildings, which stood across and askew from each other, or in the same Chase ATM lobby on Seventy-ninth, or in the late-night Korean shop collecting, if you were Zwelish, a pack of cigarettes, or, if you were Blondy, a bottle of ginger beer or a packet of wasabi peanuts. Or, most stirringly, far from the block they shared, at adjacent bookstalls in Union Square on a hot Saturday noon, where they honored the strangeness of detecting each other so far afield with a curt nod. That nod could have been the whole of it. But Blondy didn't play by the Manhattan-neighbor rules. He was provocative, voluble, grabby. He collected life histories, he'd once bragged to me, of the block's fleet of dog-walkers, maypoled in leashes on their way to the park, confused to be approached when nearly anyone else would switch pavements to get a berth from roiling terriers. Cooed at strollered babies until lonely Tibetan nannies, the invisible persons of Manhattan, practically swooned in his long arms. Blondy regaled waiters, too; I'd seen him do it.

Anyway, Alan Zwelish, short, muscled, his eyes sparkling with suspicion, sports coats pixied with dandruff, became a fascination. Bearded when Blondy first noticed him, Zwelish shaved within a year or so, revealing features younger and grimmer than Blondy had guessed, a knuckly chin and somewhat sensuous lips. Tenured-professorial in the pretentious facial hair, without it Zwelish was revealed to be no more than thirty-five. His Bogart smoking mannerisms seemed the result of mirror study and, like the renounced beard, an attempt to gain control of the lower portion of his face. Blondy watched this proud, drum-tight personality fidget past him on the street and began projecting; he couldn't help it: an unfinished degree in journalism, concerned married sisters in New Jersey or Connecticut (but probably New Jersey), weights but no cardio, aggrieved blind dates, *Cigar Aficionado* and *Stereophile,* takeout menus, acres of porn.

What was positive was this: Zwelish owned his apartment, the basement of a co-oped town house, and made a living consulting on business software—these facts Blondy got out of Alan Zwelish, semi-voluntarily, the first time he introduced himself, on Seventy-eighth Street.

The next time they passed, Zwelish attempted to look the other way, as though offering up this information had been a paying of dues, and he could now revert to nodding acquaintance. No dice, not with Blondy, who launched one of his in-medias-res gambits (the equivalent, maybe, of a Max Frisch questionnaire): The parrots were missing, had Zwelish heard? What? Zwelish hadn't ever seen the flock of green parrots, rumored to be pets escaped over the years, which congregated in certain trees on York Avenue at Seventy-seventh, around which you could hear a tropical cloud of parrot conversation? These birds were a totem of the neighborhood; it was essential Zwelish see them. But Blondy hadn't managed to spot them for more than a week. Was Zwelish doing anything urgent at the moment, or would he join Blondy for a walk to search them out? Incredibly—or not, given Blondy's charismatic sway—Zwelish excused himself for a moment to put his briefcase inside and take a leak, then rejoined Blondy, and they strolled together to York. It was a perfect afternoon, a temperate wind rebounding off the river. They found the parrots easily. (Whether they'd ever been missing at all Zwelish was left to wonder.)

Now the hard little man had been cracked open. As

Sigismund Blondy saw him, Zwelish walked in a fiery aura of loneliness, but Blondy had gotten inside the penumbra. Zwelish would grab Blondy on the street and describe family plights: the barely tolerated Passover at his—yes!—sister's in New Jersey, the difficulty of properly liquidating his father's gnarled-up assets, which were under his elderly mom's watch. And brag, essentially. Was Blondy drinking the crap water that came out of the Seventy-eighth Street taps? He should install such-and-such purification system in his sink. Cash sitting in a money-market account was as good as thrown away; Zwelish was in certain arcane tech stocks and had also acquired a Motherwell print. Blondy was invited to an East Hampton guesthouse weekend? That place was hell, trust Zwelish. Zwelish's high-school buddy had a place in the Berkshires, a better value. Blondy *rented*? Hopeless! Everything was a competition in which Blondy wouldn't compete, saying, "Look at who you're talking to, Alan. I'm like the parrots, just roosting here, decorating the area. I'd rather leave nothing behind but delicious memories." Bohemian standards Zwelish wouldn't ratify. "You're a fool," he'd say. "Yes," Blondy agreed, "I'm a fool, exactly." Zwelish narrowed his eyes. "But you don't know how dangerous it is to be a fool. Dangerous to yourself and others." Blondy thought, What others?

Possibly Zwelish meant the women. Sigismund Blondy, like any tall dissolute specimen, had women around him, in roles likely unclarified even to themselves: exes, friends, liaisons. Zwelish witnessed a certain number of the comings and goings of this elegant flock, which culminated in an introduction at a First Avenue Greek diner during morning hours suggestive of an overnight visit, before collaring Blondy alone one day to say, "Okay, Sig, how do you do it?"

"Do what?"

"Five different women I've seen you with in the past two months."

"Friends, Alan, those are my friends."

Zwelish crushed his cigarette under his running shoe, the way he wanted to stub out Blondy's line of defense. "Don't bullshit me. I see them lean into you. That's not friends."

"When you reach my age, women lean into you for a variety of reasons."

"I could use some friends like that."

Blondy felt he'd been offered a significant confidence. Insouciant as he was, he hadn't ever felt that he could quite ask a man as unattractive as Zwelish how he made do. Before any tenderness broke out between them, however, Zwelish thrust a knife in. "I've seen you hitting on those illiterate babysitters, too. The whole block talks about it, you know."

This prospect tipped Blondy back on his heels for an instant: that he, who prided himself on his panoramic insight into Seventy-eighth Street, could be under the microscope himself. And, using that instant, Zwelish made his escape.

*

A bruising friendship, if it was one. And, like Blondy and me at the movies, many weeks could pass between encounters. Did Blondy only fantasize that Zwelish peered out of his basement window slats deciding whether or not, on a given afternoon, he wanted to see Blondy? In any case, when they did meet, Zwelish generally seemed to have some willful challenge ready, as if he prepared with flash cards. "Not awake yet?" if he saw Blondy with coffee in the afternoon. "Never awake at all anymore," Blondy would say, always willing to play the decrepit jester, the has-been, hoping he could un-push Zwelish's buttons. "Want a job, Blondy? You should write an opera about Donald Trump. He's what passes for a hero these days!" Blondy didn't compose operas, but never mind. Still, after Zwelish's initial remark they'd often fall into the earlier style of more relaxed banter. And Zwelish sometimes let his guard down and complained, obscurely, about "modern urban women." He'd only gloss the topic, and Blondy didn't press at the sore point. Zwelish seemed to know how vulnerable Zwelish wanted to get.

"Can't you get one of those babysitters to do your laundry for you?" Zwelish said one day when he saw Blondy humping a Santa Clausian bag to the Chinese dry cleaner. Zwelish seemed particularly keen and chipper, and rolled up his sleeve to show off a nicotine patch. More bragging. He explained that he'd already stepped down two patch levels, after fifteen years of pack-a-day smoking.

"I never thought of this before," said Blondy, "but if you *wanted* to smoke but were having trouble getting started, the patch could really do the trick, couldn't it?"

"What are you talking about?"

"If you wanted to be a smoker," Blondy said, explicating the joke. "You could step up instead of down." Zwelish brought out his silly side; he couldn't help it. "Once you get to the top level, you tear off that patch and—voilà!—you'd want a cigarette *urgently*."

"Fuck you," Zwelish said, and walked away. His self-improvements were apparently no laughing matter.

Yet Sigismund Blondy, being who he was, found Zwelish all the more precious for his touchiness. He constituted a test that Blondy, who'd sledded on pure charm through so many controversies, couldn't pass. He adored Zwelish for causing him, at this late date, to want to do better, try harder, give more.

It was months later that the real opportunity came: Alan Zwelish's definitive self-renovation, one that Blondy instantly vowed to treat only reverently, beatifically. Zwelish returned from a mysterious trip in possession of an Asian wife. Blondy heard it first from another neighbor (shades of "the whole block knows"), who included a nosy speculation as to whether the union had been made by online advertisement or some other mechanical arrangement, before he saw her for himself. From Vietnam, it was revealed when they met on the street, and tiny enough to make Zwelish look tall. Doris, Zwelish introduced her as, though he later confided that her name was something else, Do Lun or Du Lan. Bright dark eyes and features so precise they seemed tooled. At this first meeting Blondy clasped Zwelish's hand, took his elbow, gave his warmest congratulations. Almost bent to kiss Doris, but thought better. She was too self-contained and skittish, a cipher. Zwelish pulled her close to him, seeming for once immune to hurt, a being formed only of pride and delight. Blondy was a part of the family, if only because at the moment anyone, even a passing stranger, would have been. Blondy watched them disappear into the basement apartment, Zwelish gallantly rushing past Doris to unlock the gate, and felt a disproportionate happiness, one he suspected he'd have to make an effort to conceal.

Zwelish never attacked Blondy now, his sarcasm apparently totally evaporated, and if Blondy ever experimented with a teasing joke (calling Doris "Mrs. Z"), it seemed to go right over Zwelish's head. Or under it, as if the man were floating. They'd greet each other heartily, with or without Doris in Zwelish's tow. It was as though Zwelish had advertised the director to Doris in advance as a sterling friend, a local pillar, and then so invested in the notion that he forgot his old wariness. Doris, when she was along, watched carefully. Her English wasn't hopeless, once you pierced the gauze of the almost total deference she showed her husband, never speaking without checking his eyes for cues. Who knew what else she was capable of, what life she'd led before, what life she'd expected coming here. Zwelish, who worked increasingly from home, who made fewer consulting trips out of town, kept her attached at the hip.

Soon enough Doris's pregnancy was noticeable on her scrawny frame. Her posture was too good to hide it past the third month. Zwelish accepted these congratulations, too, but distantly. This was a cold winter, everyone battened into woolen layers and readily excused from dawdling in the open, and Zwelish and his expectant young wife were more and more like figures in a snow globe, viewable but uncontactable from the human realm. They didn't seem happy or unhappy, just curled into each other, whispering on the street, a totally opaque domestic unit. Blondy couldn't get a rise or anything else out of Zwelish, and I knew Blondy well enough to feel how this irked him. It explained the reckless choice he made. Likely, given his history with Zwelish already, Blondy knew it was reckless, though he did it wholly in gentleness and out of sheer enthusiasm. One day when Doris was five or six months along and spring had broken out on the street, Blondy ran into her alone as she returned, waddling slightly, from the Korean market. He insisted on carrying her plastic bags to the door of the basement apartment.

This was bad enough, really, since it wasn't beyond Zwelish's established range to feel this as a rebuke for not having accompanied Doris to the store. But worse, much worse, at the door Blondy reached under Doris's sweater and T-shirt, not without asking first, and cupped his palm underneath the globe that burgeoned there. He did it elegantly—nothing but elegance, with a woman especially, was possible for Blondy. Doris wasn't jarred. Blondy didn't linger. Just felt it and murmured something about "a miracle," and something else about "lucky Alan." Asked "Boy or girl?" and Doris told him: "Boy."

Zwelish, who'd heard their voices and come to the window, now rushed out, unlocked the gate, and pulled Doris inside. He seemed to have some imprecation caught in his throat, which produced a kind of angry hiccup as he glared up at Blondy. Then, with his wife, he was gone.

Conveniently, Zwelish was alone when he next met Blondy on the street. He lowered his shoulder as they came near each other, and when Blondy said his name, he squared and delivered a sour look. "What do you want from me?" he asked Blondy. "Nothing you wouldn't want to give" was Blondy's reply.

"Why'd you call me 'lucky'?" Zwelish asked.

"What?"

" 'Lucky Alan.' What's that supposed to mean?"

"Nothing," Blondy said, exhausted at last.

"Then why don't you just keep your distance." Zwelish exited on the line.

Now came the deep valley in their relations, though Blondy somehow never doubted it would eventually be crossed. Weeks or a month could go by without their passing on the street, and words were never spoken. Blondy was busy then, in the effort that included our own first meeting, the Koch plays. The boy was born, and the little triad was sighted on Seventy-eighth Street, always self-reliant and self-contained, always in a hurry. And, finally, Blondy uncovered the existence of the "whole block"; it consisted of an older woman (meaning, I guessed, Blondy's age) living in Blondy's own building, whom Blondy mainly identified with a boring dispute over recycling, and who, it turned out, was eagerly running him down to absolutely anyone, from the market Koreans to new tenants; to the dog-walkers she'd interrogate after their talks with Blondy, as if deprogramming them; to, presumably, Zwelish. One of the dog-walkers, the most garrulous and multifariously connected (he walked the Jack Russell and the corgis and the aging dachshund), spilled it all to Blondy at last. And also said that Zwelish himself had once halted on the sidewalk to take part in the latest Blondy-trashing session. That Zwelish had said he'd never trusted Blondy, was "always just playing along," whatever that meant. As though Blondy's affection were so pernicious it had to be negotiated with.

In the earlier months of this stalemate, Blondy had spotted Zwelish with or without his new family four or five times, then Doris alone with the boy in a stroller two or three others. Blondy hadn't noticed to what degree he'd pridefully withdrawn from the daily life of the block (this would have been the period of the great escalation in my multiplex encounters with Blondy, when we most frequently "accidentally" rendezvoused and ended up at wine bars) until the garrulous dog-walker stopped him and delivered the news: Alan Zwelish had died, suddenly, of an inoperable brain tumor, discovered only weeks before it killed him. Doris and the child had inherited whatever he had, and an insurance claim was going to keep them in the apartment across the street. Here was the full horror of a relationship that both relied on chance meetings and was subject to utter estrangement: what you could miss in an interval. In this case, the whole end.

There was only one possible choice at the news. Blondy rushed to the apartment to see Doris. She let him in. Entering Zwelish's lair for the first time ever, seeing—yes!—the high-end audio equipment and the pile of free weights, as well as the framed Motherwell, and most of all the one-year-old playing in a folding crib littered with the plush toys he suspected were Zwelish's handpicked tokens of adoration, made Blondy's heart righteous, as if confirmation of his old guesses proved the claims Zwelish had always refused. Doris sat across from him, rigid in her chair, eyes dry. She offered him nothing, and he didn't approach her, or the child—this wasn't a visit, it was a reckoning. He started with the only words to start with, "I'm sorry," meant as an overture to the explanations he wanted to offer whether Doris cared or understood. But she had a clarification of her own to make, one that threw his motives into irrelevancy.

"I'm glad he's gone."

Blondy hadn't misheard. Her syntax was exact and unmistakable, despite the accent. The sentiment laid bare.

"Why?"

"He never let me go anywhere." Doris's tone was angry, the feeling fresh. "We only fighted all day."

Blondy just nodded, needed no prompting to accept the truth of this account.

"I didn't love Alan. Now we"—she turned, to make Blondy understand she included the boy—"have this. Much better."

Blondy began weeping, openly, pouring out stuff he didn't know was inside, matters of his fear of death generally, as well as rage at Alan Zwelish for having pushed him away and at himself for having let himself be pushed.

"You cry," Doris said, not cruelly.

*

Having been chosen or volunteered to receive the confession from Blondy that Doris Zwelish had preempted, I fastened on the real-estate implications. They seemed to me not inconsiderable, given Blondy's Seventy-eighth Street rent stabilization. "Your response was to move from the block?"

"I couldn't confront the recycling lady, to begin with," Blondy said. "Let alone watch Doris raising the kid before my eyes—what if he came out looking like Alan? The block wasn't mine anymore. I was like a zombie—they'd be right to shun me after a while. I was embarrassed for myself, but also for Zwelish. Nobody could forget him if I didn't go."

"So it was altruistic, moving away?"

"*Necessary,* Grahame."

Again I felt a paranoiac certainty that in telling his

tale Sigismund Blondy had enlisted me in a theatrical invention—cast me in a role—for the benefit of an unknown audience, perhaps only himself. There was no Alan Zwelish, or Alan Zwelish had never married or died: The whole episode was confabulation. For an instant I wanted to go to the library and dig for an obituary. But then I knew that the story was true. Inventing a smoker who'd quit and then succumbed to cancer was beneath Blondy. No, my feeling of unreality was a sympathetic response, not a clue to a lie: I'd been infected with Blondy's own fear, that grandiosity had made his human self specious—a *zombie*. He fled Seventy-eighth Street afraid he'd made it a stage for theatrics. In his nightmares he might have heard this accusation, delivered in the recycling lady's voice: not that he was molesting nannies but that he treated others as figures in a shadow play.

The moment I suspected this horror I wanted to assuage it, by speaking of his true and inexpressible feelings for Zwelish. "You don't choose who you love, Sigismund."

Blondy looked relieved that I was chasing a moral in his fable, rather than staring with him into the black hole of his personality. "I like that," he mused. "You don't choose who you love. Or who loves you. *That* was Alan's problem."

"No wonder he was pissed. Whatever he was searching for, nothing could have made him expect *you*."

"Ha!"

I'd have done anything for Blondy at that moment,

and, correspondingly, I loathed Alan Zwelish, though I knew there was more Zwelish than Blondy in me, which was likely the reason I was seated here. I hated Zwelish for showing Blondy death, just as I'd hate a teenager for informing a five-year-old that Santa Claus was a fake. I hoped Blondy would live to a thousand, for revenge.

"Let us assume that you have never killed another human being. How do you account for it?"

"Sorry?"

"That's the next question." Blondy had unfolded his photocopies again. "Or this: *Which would you rather do: die or live on as a healthy animal? Which animal?"*

The King of Sentences

This was the time when all we could talk about was sentences, sentences—nothing else stirred us. Whatever happened in those days, whatever befell our regard, Clea and I couldn't rest until it had been converted into what we told ourselves were astonishingly unprecedented and charming sentences: "Esther's cleavage is something to be noticed" or "You can't have a contemporary prison without contemporary furniture" or "I envision an art which will make criticism itself seem like a cognitive symptom, one which its sufferers define to themselves as taste but is in fact nothing of the sort" or "I said I want my eggs scrambled, not destroyed." At the explosion of such a sequence from our green young lips, we'd rashly scribble it on the wall of our apartment with a filthy wax pencil, or type it twenty-five times on the same sheet of paper and then photocopy the paper twenty-five times and then slice each page into twenty-five slices on the paper cutter in the photocopy shop and then scatter the resultant six hundred and twenty-five slips of paper throughout the streets of our city, fortunes without cookies.

We worked in bookstores, the only thing to do. Nobody who didn't—and that included every one of our customers—knew what any of the volumes throbbing along those shelves was worth, not remotely. Nor did the bookstores' owners. Clea and I were custodians of a treasury of sentences much bigger on the inside than on the outside. Though we mostly handled the books only by their covers (or paged briefly through to ascertain that no dunce had striped the pages yellow or pink with a Hi-Liter), we communed deeply with them, felt certain that only we deserved to abide with them. Any minute we'd read them all cover to cover, it was surely about to happen. Meanwhile, every customer robbed us a little. At the cash registers we spoke sentences tailored to convey our disdain, in terms so subtle it was barely detectable. If our customers blinked a little at the insults we embedded in our thank-yous, we believed they just might be worthy of the marvels their grubby dollars entitled them to bear away.

We disparaged modern and incomplete forms: gormless and garbled jargon, graffiti, advertising, text-messaging.

No sentence conveyed by photons or bounced off satellites had ever come home intact. Punctuation! We knew it was holy. Every sentence we cherished was sturdy and biblical in its form, carved somehow by hand-dragged implement or slapped onto sheets by an inky key. For sentences were sculptural, were we the only ones who understood? Sentences were bodies, too, as horny as the flesh-envelopes we wore around the house all day. Erotically enjambed in our loft bed, Clea patrolled my utterances for subject, verb, predicate, as a chef in a five-star kitchen would minister a recipe, ensuring that a soufflé or sourdough would rise. A good brave sentence ("I can hardly bear your heel at my nape without roaring") might jolly Clea to instant climax. We'd rise from the bed giggling, clutching for glasses of cold water that sat in pools of their own sweat on bedside tables. The sentences had liberated our higher orgasms, nothing to sneeze at. Similarly, we were also sure that sentences of the right quality could end this hideous endless war, if only certain standards were adopted at the higher levels. They never would be. All the media trumpeted the administration's lousy grammar.

But we were chumps and we knew it. As makers of sentences we were practically fetal, beneath notice, unlaunched, fooling around in our spare time or on somebody else's dime. Nobody loved our sentences as we loved them, and so they congealed or grew sour on our tongues. We barely glanced at our wall-scribblings for fear of what a few weeks or even hours might expose in our infatuations. Our photocopied fortune slips we'd find in muddy clogs in storm drains, tangled with advertising flyers, unheeded. Our manuscripts? Those were unspeakable secrets, kept not only from the world but from each other. My pages were shameful, occluded everywhere with xxxxxx's of regret. I scurried to read Clea's manuscript every time she left the apartment but never confessed that I even knew it existed. Her title was *Those Young Rangers Thought Love Was a Scandal Like a Bald White Head*. Mine was *I Heard the Laughter of the Sidemen from Behind Their Instruments*.

Others might hail kings of beer or burgers—we bowed to the King of Sentences. There was just one. We owned his titles in immaculate firsts and tattered reading copies and odd variant editions. It thrilled us to see the pedestrian jacket copy and salacious cover art on his early mass-market paperbacks: to think that he'd once been considered fodder for dime-store carousels! The newest editions of the titles he'd allowed to be reprinted (four early novels had been suppressed from republication) were splendidly austere, their jackets, from the small presses that published him now, bearing text only, no graven images. The progress of his editions on our shelf was like a cartoon of evolution, a slug crawling from the surf to become a mammal, a monkey, and then at last a hairless noble fellow gazing into the future.

The King of Sentences gave no interviews, taught nowhere, condescended to appear at no panels or symposia. His tastes, hobbies, and heartbreaks were unknown, and we extrapolated them from his books at our peril.

His digital footprint was pale: people like that didn't care about people like him. Google, for what it was worth, favored a famous painter of wildlife scenes—beaver dams, heron hideaways—with the same name. The King of Sentences only wrote, beavering away himself on a dam of quintessence, while wholly oblivious of public indifference and of a sales record by now likely descending to rungs occupied by poets. His author photograph, identical on twenty years of jackets and press clippings until it stopped circulating at all, arrested him somewhere in the mid-sixties, turtlenecked, holding a cocktail glass forever. His last cocktail, maybe.

In the same loft where we entangled, Clea and I drove ourselves mad reading the King of Sentences's books aloud, by candlelight, when we ought to have been sleeping. We'd tear the book from each other's hands for the pleasure of running his words like gerbils in the habitrails of our own mouths. We'd alternate chapters, pages, paragraphs, finally sentences, at last agree to read him in unison. He could practically hear us as we intoned his words, we'd swear they reached his ears. But not really. Really, we were vowing to ourselves and to each other that we'd make a day trip in search of the King of Sentences, that we'd flush him out, propel ourselves into his company and confidence, buoy him with our love and bind ourselves (and our secret manuscripts, oh yeah!) to his greatness. We each had what the other needed, of this we were positive. Maybe we'd watch him write. Maybe he'd watch us dance, or fuck, who knew? We'd buy him lunch. He was surely mortal enough for lunch. He'd want us at least for lunch.

He lived, we'd learned, north of the city, having drawn from his days as a Greenwich Village flaneur whatever inspiration he'd needed, and departed around the time of that last photograph and cocktail. (We figured that his departure from the narrow town house on Jane Street marked an expiration date on anything west of Second Avenue as an authentic locale.) Minimal detective work pinned him to a P.O. box in Hastings-on-Hudson—how clever and coy he had been to find a place-name that was itself, with the mere insertion of an apostrophe, a sentence, and a faintly lascivious one, too. So it was that we knew he'd summoned us to his hiding place: Clea could play Hudson, and I'd be Hasting.

We sent a postcard warning, addressed to his box. No return address, so he couldn't refuse. No fancy sentences, fearing his judgment of those. Just fragments: "coming in two weeks," "get ready," "can't wait to meet in person" (as if we'd already met on other planes, for we had). The appointed day came upon us like a sickness, and though each in our privacy might have preferred to stay in bed and sweat it out we couldn't have looked each other in the eye if we hadn't staggered out of doors, to the subway, up to Grand Central Terminal. During the short ride we held hands, fever-sweaty at the palms. Exiting Metro-North's Hastings-on-Hudson station under a thundercloud-clotted sky, we found ourselves the sole

travelers not claimed by family members waiting in
Subarus or beeping their driver-side doors unlocked as
they crossed the parking lot with cell phones clammed to
their ears. The train continued on behind us, and the station depopulated as if neutron-bombed.

"This is the town of the King of Sentences."

"This little town."

"He could be watching us now, don't act stupid. With
a telescope."

We blundered along something called Main Street,
seeking the post office, until a passerby directed us to
Warburton Avenue. Inside the mediocre lobby we staked
out a position near the numbered boxes, innocuously pretending to screw up our change-of-address forms so that
we had to start over again a dozen times. His box, which
we surveilled with peripheral vision only, pulsed with risk
and possibility—our own postcard had been handled
there, a precursor to this encounter.

Losing patience, we sidled to the main counter. "What
time on the average day does the boxholder typically, you
know, pick up?"

"Box mail goes up at ten thirty."

"Right, sure, but mostly when do citizens appear and
begin to gather it up, take it to their private homes?"

"Whenever they care to."

"Sure, right, this is America, isn't it?"

"Sure is."

"Thank you."

We resumed charades with the chained pen. Two, three, five, eight, eighteen Hastings-on-Hudsonians lumbered in to check their boxes, sort circulars into recycling bins, greet the postmistress, and trade coins for stamps, each of comically tiny denominations. Everyone in this hamlet, it seemed, had just found a sixteen- or twenty-three-cent stamp in a dusty drawer, and had chosen today to supplement it up to viability using car-seat nickels and pennies.

Yet somehow between transactions the postmistress had snuck away for a tattling phone call, or so we surmised from the blinking patrol car that now swept up in front of the P.O. Into the lobby strode a cowboyesque figure, a man, late-fiftyish, wearing a badge in the manner of a star, lean and, when he spoke, laconic. Clea read my mind, saying, "You the sheriff in these parts?"

"Chief of police."

"Not the sheriff of Hastings-on-Hudson?"

"No, ma'am, there isn't one. Can I ask what you're doing here?"

"Waiting."

"Have you folks got postal business today?"

"No," I said. "But we've got business with someone who might have postal business, if that's okay."

"I suppose it might be, sir, but I'm forced to wonder who we're talking about."

"The King of Sentences."

"I see. You wouldn't happen to be the authors of a certain unsigned and borderline-ominous postcard?"

"Might happen to be, though there was hardly ominous intent."

"I see. And now you're waiting, I'm guessing, for the addressee."

"In the manner of free Americans in a federally controlled public space, yes. We checked with the postmistress."

"I see. You mind if I wait a bit myself?"

"By definition we can't."

Soon enough he appeared. The King of Sentences, unmistakably, though withered like a shrunken-apple fetish of the noble cipher in the photograph. He wore a gray sweatshirt and caramel corduroys with the knees and thighs bald, like a worn radial tire. Absurd black Nikes over gray dress socks. Hair white and scant. Eyes tiny and darting. They darted to the not-sheriff, who nodded minimally. The King nodded back with equal economy.

We collapsed, as planned, to our knees, conveying the beautiful anguish of our subjection to the sole King of Sentences—bowed heads, fingers wriggling as if combing the air for particles of his greatness. A chapter of *I Heard the Laughter of the Sidemen from Behind Their Instruments,* secreted in the waistband of my underwear, buckled as I knelt there. The King stood inert, if anything sagged slightly. The chief turned and shook his head, a little appalled.

"You okay?" he asked the King.

"Sure. Let me talk to them a minute."

"Anything you say." The law went outside, to stand and

take a cigarette beside his cruiser. He watched us through the window. We nodded and waved as we scrambled back to our feet.

"Who sent you?" the King said.

"You, you, you," Clea said. "It was you."

"We weren't so much sent as drawn," I said. "You gave us the gift of your work, and now we're here, a gift in return."

"Take us," Clea said.

"No, thank you," the King said. His eyes shifted nervously from Clea, settling on me.

"We anointed you the King of Sentences," I told him. "We're the ones who did that. Nobody else." I didn't want to bully him with news of how scarcely his name circulated, how stale and marked-down the assembly of his hardcovers on used-bookstore shelves.

"I didn't tell you to come."

"No, but you are responsible for our presence."

"Let me be clear. I have nothing for you."

"Take us home."

"Not on your life."

"We came all this way."

He shrugged. "When's the next train back?"

The sentences that emerged from his mouth were flayed, generic, like lines from black-and-white movies. I tried not to be disappointed in this stylistic turn. He had something to teach us, always.

"We don't care. We don't have tickets. We came for you."

"I don't fraternize. This kind of intrusion is the last thing I need."

"Lunch," I begged. "Just lunch."

"I eat only what my housekeeper prepares. A disproportion of sodium could murder me at this point."

Clea hugged herself with pleasure. I heard her murmur the line, cherishing it privately, ". . . disproportion . . . sodium . . . murder me." The King craned on his Nike toes, checking that the cop was still outside.

"Forget lunch. An hour of your time."

"We're to hover in the post-office lobby for an hour? Doing what, exactly?"

"No, let's go somewhere," Clea said. "A hotel room, if you won't have us in your house."

"Or the bar," I said, offering a check on Clea's presumption. "The bar in the lobby of a hotel, a public setting. For a cocktail."

The King laughed for the first time, a cackle edged, like a burned cookie, with bitterness. "What largesse. You'd take me to one of our town's fine hotels. They're as superb as the restaurants. Motel 6 or Econo Lodge, I believe those are your options."

"Anywhere," Clea panted.

The King's weary gaze again shunted: Clea, myself, the disinterested postmistress, the chief outside, who now ground a butt into the curb with his heel and turned his head to follow the progress of some retreating buttocks. The King's voice edged down an octave. "Econo Lodge," he said. "On Lower Brunyon. I'll find you there in fifteen minutes."

"We don't have a vehicle."

"Too bad."

"Can we ride with you?"

"No way, José."

"How do we get there?"

"Figure it out." The King of Sentences departed the P.O. and skulked around the corner and out of view, presumably to his car. I couldn't have entirely imagined the extra little kick in his step as he went. The King had been energized, if only slightly, by meeting his subjects. It was a start, I thought.

On the sidewalk we teetered with excitement, blinking in the glare that now filtered through the gnarled clouds. The chief looked us up and down again. We offered charming smiles.

"Can I give you folks a lift back to the station?"

"No, thanks, we're looking for Lower Brunyon. Care to point us in the right direction?"

"Why Lower Brunyon?"

"The Econo Lodge, if you must know. Is it walking distance?"

"Longish, I'd say. Why not let me escort you?"

"Sure."

We sat behind a cage. The backseat smelled of smoke, perfume, and vomit, raising interesting questions about the definition of police work in Hastings-on-Hudson. The chief took corners smoothly, in the prowling, snaky manner of a driver unconcerned about regulating his speed.

"You two in the regular habit of doing junk like this?"

"What do you mean by 'junk'?"

"Putting yourselves in the hands of a customer like your friend in there?"

"I'd be junk in his hands any day," Clea said defiantly.

"Well, he's old and likely pretty harmless by now," the chief said. "I saw him the other day in the pharmacy, getting himself one of those inflatable doughnuts for sitting on when you've got anal discomfort. I'd say from what I've heard those sort of troubles are his just deserts. We're not dummies around here, you know. When he moved up here from the city, a certain number of stories trailed after him. He's been a bad boy."

"He's the greatest maker of sentences in the United States of America," I said.

"I've had a look," the chief said. "He's not bad. I'm just wondering if you ever troubled with the content of his books, as opposed to just the sentences."

"Sentences *are* content," Clea said.

The chief lifted his hands in mock surrender. "Fair enough then, I've said my piece. Just understand this— whatever my personal views of either his character or his prose, he's under my protection surely as any other citizen in this town. *Comprende?*"

"Does everyone up here speak Spanish? Is this a bilingual metropolis?" Clea said.

"That's enough out of you, young lady. Here's the Econo Lodge, and a good day to you both."

"Thanks, Chief."

We crept inside the Econo Lodge's slumbering atrium. A uniformed teenage clerk blinked hello, raised his hand. We ignored him. The King of Sentences hovered beside a counter bearing urns of complimentary coffee labeled "Premium," "Diesel," and "Jet Fuel." The King nodded mutely, beckoned to us with a tilt of his chin. We trailed him down a corridor with a tongue-hued carpet. I worked not to visualize an anal doughnut.

"Inside," he said.

The King lit only a lamp at the bedside in the windowless room. We crowded in, the room a mere margin to the queen-size bed. The air conditioner rumbled and hummed. The temperature was frigid. The King took the only chair, gestured us to the bed's edge. We sat.

Clea and I began simultaneously, tangling aloud. "We're—" I said. Clea said, "You're the—"

"Let's not waste time," the King interrupted. He spoke in an exhausted snarl, all redemptive possibility purged from his voice and manner. Our rendezvous had taken on the starkness of an endgame. "Do you want money?"

"Money?" I said.

"That's right." He reached into his shirt pocket and revealed a packet of twenties, obviously prepared in advance. It occurred to me wildly that he'd taken us for blackmailers. Perhaps he was blackmailed routinely, had cash on hand for regular payouts. "How much will it take to make you go away?" He began counting out piles: "Twenty, forty, sixty, eighty, one hundred, twenty, forty, sixty, eighty, two hundred—"

"We don't want your money!" I nearly shouted. "You've given us enough, you've given us everything! We're here to give something back!"

"I suppose I'm meant to be glad to hear it." He repocketed his money carelessly.

"We'd like you to be glad, yes."

He only cocked an eyebrow. "What have you got for me?"

I untucked my polo shirt and withdrew my chapter, the pages a mass curled and baked in its secret compression against my belly.

"I knew you looked funny!" Clea cried. I ignored her, handed the pages across to the King. He accepted them, his expression sour.

"For a moment there I thought you were about to undress," he said.

"Would you like that?" Clea blurted. "Should we undress?"

The King examined us starkly. He placed my chapter ignominiously on the carpet beneath his chair. Perhaps now we were at the crossroads, perhaps we had his attention at last. "Yes," he said cautiously. "I think that could be . . . advantageous."

We stripped, racing to be the first bared to his view. I'd lose the race either way, for Clea had rigged the game: She had written a sentence on her stomach in blue marker.

The sorcerer lately couldn't recall whether he was a capable sleeper or an insomniac. Brilliant, I thought bitterly. The King stared. I saw Clea's pubic hair through the eyes of the King. Clea's bush was full and crazy. I thought, I will never see it again without seeing the pubic hair at which the King of Sentences once glanced. The King said, "Insomniac, I believe."

Clea blushed around the sentence, her flesh blazing like neon.

"Hand me your clothes, please."

We handed the King our clothes. He began immediately rending them, in a weary frenzy of destruction, tearing both of our shirts sleeve from sleeve, shredding Clea's bra and underwear, slicing at her skirt with his nicotine teeth. He struggled to do any damage to my jeans. I felt I wanted to help him somehow, but stood jellied in my nakedness, doing nothing, not wishing to insult him, to draw attention to his feebleness. It was a mighty enough display, given his age. The hands that had forged the supreme sentences in contemporary American writing were now dismembering the syntax of my underwear.

Soon enough our daily costumes lay in an unseemly ruined pile at our feet. My chapter scattered beneath the clothes and chair legs, forgotten. He hadn't looked at even one sentence, never would. I knew I would have to forgive him. So I did it right then and there: I forgave him.

The King moved to the door. We stood in our bare feet, wobbling slightly, goose-pimpled, still breathing out clouds of expectation like frost-breath.

"That's all?" Clea said.

"That's all, you ask? Yes, that's all. That's more than enough."

"You're leaving us here."

"I am."

He closed the door carefully, not slamming it. Clea and I waited an appropriate interval, then turned and clung to each other in a kind of rapture. Understanding, abruptly and at last, just what it takes to be King. How much, in the end, it actually costs.

Traveler Home

1.

Traveler waking. Journey begins. No dreams this night. Bags packed before sunset, sink emptied, alarm rings, Traveler hits snooze, thinks snooze-lose, lies awake instead, lingering for second alarm. Quandary of toothbrush solved, laid on briefcase for ease of notforgetting. Haunted angle in morning light, toothbrush a sundial suggesting. New direction in morning light. No path more ideal than any other given. Night's snow fallen, obliterated traces. Shovel itself buried. Car in plowed mound, couldn't specify where. Drive to resume in spring's melting. Needs speak with Plowman, demand Plowman present a bill. Snowball's chance. Confrontation delayed, striding up path hopeless. Arrive baked items in hand if possible. Hardly so. Plowman's house itself irretrievable. Cars tumbled in clotted curb's-cake, ridged ice walls visible from space, satellite's eye. Path glimpsed no more lately. Plowman growing hydroponic greenhouse food, relying solely on Plowman's powers, plow's battery and headlamps undying. Plowman homeschooling Plowman's beautiful daughters. Seven dark-haired, order of height. Out of sight, in mind. Traveler alone. Traveler pining. Traveler waking, turns out dreaming. Lost tickets. Automatic coffee. Toothbrush unfound. Angle of daylight. Snows grows. Snows lose. Missing shoes. Mossy rooted path. Bridge fallen. Asteroid shower. Traveler waking. Double dreaming. Dream shakes off, a second skin, dog's wet fur. Alarm furious, astounded interval between first waking and five-minute snoozed. Traveler showering. Toothbrush foamed. Thermos brimful. Journey under way.

2.

Traveler sits watching television alone. Not alone, with Terrier. Huddled on sofa with Terrier in dark house, furnace beneath floorboards rumbling, outside snow falling again. Remote on couch handy. Traveler's flat-screen plasma television, hulking presence, only glow in warm-dark house in white-dark night. Terrier watching too, head cocked at motion, throaty growl at anything remotely ratlike, shadows skulking to edges of screen.

Terrier who has never caught any actual rat. Satellite dish provides Traveler with five hundred channels, at least in name, though dozens are fallow, wastes of pay-per-view, cooking, sports, cartoons. Still, forty or fifty channels of films, only a handful of those with commercials. Traveler tonight watches *Insomnia*, tale of weary detective, unsleeping, trudging through barren noon-lit landscapes in killer's pursuit. Traveler feels déjà vu, has perhaps seen this film or another like it, remake or sequel. Nonetheless trudges as detective trudges through story, camaraderie of sleepless. Night long-fallen everywhere, windows less-frequently lit by passing headlamps, now only yellow siren-flashing glow of Plowman passing. In this, his small-town country life, Traveler has learned his few scattered neighbors keep a newborn's hours, asleep at first dark, six, seven o'clock, rising at five, even four. Traveler long accustomed now to keeping his city hours, habit impossible of breaking, possibly the sole waking presence in a hundred-mile radius. Traveler and Plowman, on a night like this. Plowman scraping road, high in steaming plow's cab, watching funnels of volcanic white swirl in headlamps through widescreen of windshield. Traveler shudders.

As if snow outside invading, Traveler's screen begins defecting, digital freezing, slurry of staticky white pixels corrupting shots of insomniac detective. Traveler ignores until he can't, as picture worsens, glitching story line irretrievably. Traveler sighs. Time's come as he suspected. Satellite dish outside caked, icicles shredding signal, white stuff needs bumping off. Not the first time. Terrier needs decanting anyhow. This duty preeminent, regularly dragging Traveler outside cave of warmth, into snowfall, needs of Terrier for an earth patch to perfume. Traveler dons coat, knee boots, gloves. Terrier at door trepidatious understanding. Traveler gathers kitchen broom for knocking off accumulation from dish, freeing of signal, resumption of movie. No reason Traveler and Terrier can't be back on couch in minutes. So, outside, into the howl. Traveler tucking Terrier under arm, a protected football. Practically impossible in this height of snowfall for Terrier to find a place to squat. Find an evergreen with snow-sheltered interior, bed of cones barely dusted, best hope. Preferable to carry dog seeking ideal spot. Otherwise Terrier's low belly beads with icicles, Terrier runs discouraged frozen yelping for porch. Trial and error, Traveler now carries Terrier.

Satellite dish first. Traveler trudges hip-deep in drifts at the side of the house. Raises broom into swirl, rattles ice on heaped dish, scoops snow from concavity. Icicles clatter to shards deep in snowbank. Dish freed, adequate. Through own window like yeti peeper, Traveler spots lit screen, image rescued. Distant stratospheric signal unblocked from local occlusion of particles. Unfathomable mysteries of science best ignored. Sleepless detective restored oblivious to malfunctional interlude. Empty rooms equally oblivious, carrying on without. Now only remains the Terrier's peeing, then inside, cleave to warmth, boots-puddle melting by vent. Traveler carries dog and broom across open margin of yard, high-fall of snow, into the woods, into the trees, where canopy offers Terrier possibilities.

Traveler had in warmer months begun carving path back into woods, labor of unfamiliar intimacy with saplings, wood saws, mammoth treetop clippers. Pushing through woods, foot by foot, toward rendezvous with path already established, deep in trees, running behind all their houses invisible. Known locally as "Drunkard's Path," ribald suggestion of shitfaced farmers sneaking home concealed from judgmental porch-views. No sense how much farther to reach this older path, Traveler had simply gone on clipping, chopping, making his own mark. Provides place for Terrier to defecate anyhow. Tonight path's a white tunnel, trees large and small draped silent, cone of moonlit intensity. Traveler sets Terrier down in relative shallow, waits. Terrier alerts, snarls. Traveler looks. Ahead on path now, arrayed in woods, seven wolves. Teeth bared, snarling too, ready. The always feared. Traveler's seen animals here, sure, mostly prey, deer, bunnies. Nobody from this place would call them bunnies but he can't think of another word. Once a fox, harmlessly decorative. Eagles overhead sometimes turning, as if with Terrier in sights. Locals joke he'd best keep Terrier inside. Keep close, city dog. Now here they've come, the deeper locals. Patrolling for drunkards maybe, but they'll take what they get. Traveler thinking always danger to Terrier never to himself. Is broom enough to fend them? Then sees basket.

Wolf now emerging from back of group, padding in

white path, basket in jaws. Others part to allow this passing. Terrier still growling low in throat, wolves unimpressed. Traveler cranes to look in basket. A baby there, human animal faintly squalling. Tucked in bare blanket, lightly snow-clung. Wolf perhaps proposing a trade, baby for Terrier, as if claiming canine sovereignty here. Do they expect Traveler to eat baby? Why haven't wolves eaten baby themselves? No way to ask. Traveler as by instinct turns broom to extend handle. Wolf permits. The basket is unexpectedly light. Traveler reels it in. Wolves turn on path, scatter, not demanding Terrier or anything else in return. Terrier, idiot, goes on growling at retreating forms, as if having routed them personally. Traveler gathers basket to his arms, letting broom sink in snow. Find it later. No arm free for Terrier either, so the dog's left to hopping through snowbanks, vanishing below their height and encrusting entirely, thusly following Traveler and basket with baby onto porch, and indoors.

Baby, unwrapped indoors, is a boy baby. White blanket unstained, though even as Traveler makes this observation baby arcs yellow to moisten the basket's lining. Traveler finds towels, pats limbs dry, replaces blanket with towel, first lesson in baby's consummately blunt demands. The other being to feed. Mouth pursing in silent expectation. No question of any task but find it satisfaction. Traveler has barely anything in the fridge, much less milk. Ill-prepared for self not to mention newcomer. Should have laid in groceries before storm, Traveler's classic city-man error, now car waits for plowing, locked in driveway helpless. Plowman uncallable, ranging out in night's campaign. Likely wouldn't call if even could. Traveler's got no notion how far down he dwells on Plowman's list, but certainly low. Often plowed in dawn hours, wakes to find it done, silent reprimand of countryperson's early rising. Plowman never billing, denying Traveler ground for complaint. The times he's asked, Plowman laughs gruffly, as if Traveler's plowing is comically negligible. Then offered a rural cipher: "I'll bill when I've done enough to be worth billing." Bastard. Hence no counting on when the way might open to groceries, milk, bottles with nipples, baby food in jars if this creature's even ready for such. That mouth won't be reasoned with, won't wait, Traveler knows this much. Delves in fridge, finds one shred of dairy, a sliver of Brie. Terrier to one side watching, high whine in throat. Unhesitating on baby's behalf, Traveler carves off the cheese's white horny rind, thinking as he does how it resembles plowing the cheese like a snow-crushed road. But no time now for fruitless comparisons. Traveler frees gooey center from cheese's interior, douses in bowl with waterdrops, mashes it to yogurt-like fluid with a spoon's bottom. Dribbles mixture into waiting mouth. Baby feeds in eagerness too primal to give the name of gratitude. Naps for two hours then demands repeat. Traveler repeats. At third waking Terrier, finally bored with new rituals, pads off to curl in sleep. Baby naps, wakes, Traveler repeats. In this manner Traveler and baby manage through night's dark. Waiting for light and a path to town, doctors, grocery shelves, diapers. Outside somewhere, Plowman working.

3.

She liked to rescue dogs flung from family station wagons, Plowman's crazy eldest, whole town knows her this way, as simple as if missing a leg or with a birthmark on forehead, the crazy one. Summertime haunts the cursed bend in road where unfamiliar drivers never slow to curve's necessity, blacktop layered with curving skids, items tossed from badly secured pickups, winter a black-ice trap, regular towing work for her dad Plowman. Scored her first catch here at age fifteen: collie leaning through open back window, jumping at centrifugal careening, path of least resistance, while the family oblivious, three or four kids in backseat fighting, voices raised over dad's ballgame radio, nobody notices, poof, dog's gone. Five hundred dollar pedigreed city dog, they never even turn back, or if they do Plowman's crazy eldest has the sleek keening creature by then tied in Plowman's barn deep off main road, not a chance in the world they'd persist to find it.

She turned this anomalous event into a precedent, began vulture-like prowling vigil at road's bend in warmest weather, incredibly gathering another three dogs plopped from rolled windows in summer following, another collie to make a pair, a dachshund, comical waddler stranding in roadside ivy, and a bulldog, this last her boon companion, seen with her thenceforth everywhere, driving in cab of wretched pickup or on her infrequent town visits, in the post office or the general store, cutting across church or library lawn, defiant survivalist spinster and fist-like, oozing, snorting dog, Plowman's wild, Plowman's unfortunate, Plowman's crazy eldest daughter.

From this roadside trapping spot the other six took their license, the eldest's claim extending to her siblings. That deep-wooded bend in the road becoming a public thoroughfare in principle only, local knowledge granting the Plowman daughters' common-law provenance, a franchise, not merely a right-of-way or right-to-pass but more a right-to-halt all others who might wish to pass. Whose woods these are I think I know. Who says this is the twentieth century. Who's even asking. Where Traveler's come to make his home older ways prevail. He's learned his deference to these. On driving this road summer months Traveler's been waved over time and again, one daughter or another, despite descending age and ascending beauty impossible to keep them wholly clear when glimpsed one at a time, for coercive donation to fund of volunteer fire squad, quite possibly an imaginary force or else the daughters themselves in fire helmets, perhaps with bulldog in pickup's front seat hastening to scene, god help them all if anything ever catches fire. Or offerings of spontaneous roadside stand, equally coercive purchases of grotesque overgrown summer squash and zucchini, garden stuff that explodes in fecundity and nobody really wants to eat or knows what to do with. The local joke being lock your kitchen door in late August or the neighbors will drop off some squash. Traveler always pays, figures it's his version of a local tax, a tollbooth payment. Sums in truth absurdly small, only humiliation's payment to write off, this for Traveler easily enough accomplished.

So Traveler's only half surprised to turn the corner in snowy plowed curve of wood this morning to find himself confronted by roadblock of Plowman's daughters. Traveler taking the road at an inching crawl, lessons all long since learned, ten miles an hour to keep tires' grip on densed ice-gravel, slower still with baby in basket wedged for security behind the driver's seat, baby slumbering, drunk on Brie, tucked safe deep in terry cloth, nose and mouth solely exposed for tiny breathing. Terrier left behind in house for once. All seven daughters, first time Traveler can recall viewing entire array. Strange to glimpse even one in snowy months, with strength of local custom to hide and hibernate in winter, so many deep in woods never seen. Yet today they've come to assert their road's claim. Second-eldest daughter's hand raised coplike. No doubt of braking, at such slowness he'd hardly try to elude them, strange that such fantasies arise, no matter what dread Traveler feels at the prospect of such an encounter here. Neighbors after all. Ways of doing things, Traveler always needs recall he's the interloper by standards of five generations on same road and in same house.

Second eldest comes to driver's window as Traveler rolls down just a margin, cold being the presumable excuse for this unfriendliness. Mittened hand now in greeting raised, Traveler answers in-kind, gloveless. Second eldest a mannish-ageless woman of the woods, quite possible credible as fireman or militia captain after all, Traveler now thinks. Bearing not a trace of eldest's disarray. Other daughters hanging back, blocking road, impossible to distinguish through windshield's crystal glint, except one now he spots with rifle upright, as if at a Soviet checkpoint. Country ways. Always Traveler defers.

"Morning."

"Morning."

"Quite a night."

"Yes, and quite a day too." Traveler gestures at the white-laden trees, the sculptured lace bestowed by wind-less blizzard's passing.

"Did you by any chance hear howling in the woods last night?"

"In the woods?"

"On the Drunkard's Path, more or less."

"No howling, no."

"Wolves is the word. You better watch that little dog of yours, keep it close."

"That's what I'm always hearing, heh, yeah."

"Were you by any chance in the woods yourself for any reason?"

"Not so far in the woods as to hear any howling," Traveler says, hearing himself verge on lying. "Just to the edge for a pee, I mean of course a dog's pee. I pee in the house."

"Sure you do. Mind if I look in the car?"

"You're looking in now."

"Mind if I look a little deeper, like I'd be able to do if I, say, opened up your rear door here?"

"Well, I guess not, go ahead," Traveler saying feebly as she already had done so.

"He's here," Plowman's second eldest says and all six others come now crowding. Four in fact carry rifles, Traveler counts. Plowman's daughters in age descending, beauty ascending, the youngest the most beautiful by far Traveler helplessly confirms. If Plowman had an eighth her beauty might be dangerous, blinding, or fatal, just as well Plowman stopped at seven. This youngest now hands off her rifle, scoops baby from basket, still towel-swaddled, puts her cheek to baby's nose, then widens gap of towel at baby's mouth and thrusts baby inside her coat, where Traveler possibly glimpses bared breast before jostling of other daughters blocks any view.

Second eldest slams shut Traveler's rear door, after claiming basket. "Move along now," she says, not un-kindly.

"Sure, but first can I ask is that baby known to you already?"

"We were waiting for that baby, yes."

"So this was just a sort of wolf's wrong delivery, in effect?"

"You could say that."

"Well, I just want to do what's responsible."

"That's what you've done and you should be assured we're not in any way ungrateful. You'll want to move your car along now, you never know when there could be more traffic coming and it's hard to see very far up around that bend behind you and this is no weather for braking."

Never mind that Plowman's daughters demanded his own braking on said bend. Never mind that traffic's a comical notion around here, he wonders if they've ever seen any, these country people, how it is that they even believe they get to use the word. Never mind questions Traveler finds unspoken, like seven wolves and seven daughters, what's the story there? Questions with no way of being asked. Never mind the overnight with baby, the feeling grown between them, or at least in Traveler, hard to say what feeling baby had. Traveler wondering if baby could have stayed, grown in house, become another Traveler. Never mind, Traveler raises his hand again and rolls up the window, drives on, toward town. He needs to lay in some supplies for himself and the dog, anyway and at least.

Procedure in Plain Air

Later, after the men in jumpsuits had driven up and begun digging the hole, Stevick would remember that the guy on the bench beside him had been gazing puzzledly into the cone of his large coffee and had tried to interest him in the question of whether the café's brew aftertasted of soap or not. This day was gray, with heavy portents of rain. Not the best for sitting on the coffee shop's bench, but the interior of the café had become insufferable in all ways to Stevick: the shop's ambience and fancy name, its well-programmed iPod and fake-industrial chairs and tables and counters succeeding too completely, the room seething with overdressed-disheveled types, nerverackedly Web-surfing or doing the real-world equivalent with eye orbits through the room, every last one of whom made him feel mossy, corroded, replaced. Add to that the danger of running into his ex, Charlotte, and he never even glanced within in hope of a seat—he didn't want one. Just black, to go. He was an outdoor-bencher, he'd take his chances with the others here, backs to the shop's window, and if rain drove them off he'd have it to himself. Nor did he care to consider whether the coffee tasted of soap or not. He was getting his morning thrill on, his eye-opener, and this place, besides being on the right corner of the right block for him to stumble in, made a fine, joltingly strong concoction strictly from the addict's point of view. It could taste of lysergic acid or oysters for all he cared. Maybe every cup of coffee he'd ever drunk had tasted of soap, so he couldn't discern soap from coffee—who knew?

Stevick, meant to be job-hunting, wasn't. Too-generous severance had blurred his motivation in the months when it would have mattered. Now, season slanting to Memorial Day, the flag of Manhattan's office life was at half-mast until September. So Stevick was propped like a morning crow on that bench when the truck arrived. His front-row seat recalled to him memories of childhood puppet shows, of gazing up at the slotted stage from which Punch and Judy and their like protruded. The soapy-coffee theorist was curled over some device, brow knit, thumbs-deep in a text-message campaign, making Stevick the only witness to the disembarkment of the truck's occupants.

They parked, apparently heedlessly, in the space in front of a hydrant, but without coming nearer than three feet to the curb. Cars slowed to pass. Stevick doubted that a garbage truck could have made it through. Surely a temporary placement, a compromise, then. The vehicle was an ungainly bolted-iron thing, resembling some reconfigured laundry or diaper truck, not massive like those used for transport of money but solid enough in its way. Two men in jumpsuits popped out of the cab, and within a minute had orange traffic cones up to claim the territory that extended a few feet behind the truck, as well as between it and the curb. One contemplated the hydrant and then wryly topped it with a cone, which perched there like a dunce cap. It made an effective preemption of any indigenous neighborhood protest, an easy trump: The men in jumpsuits seemed to have some official function, even if their truck was unmarked.

The tools with which the two men dug the hole were notably quiet and efficient. After first marking a square of asphalt with yellow spray paint, using a band saw of daunting size and intensity they carved the blacktop along the lines of drying paint. At this point, Stevick's might still have been the only eyes attending. Perhaps these activities had drawn distracted, unsustained glances from a passing postal worker or nanny. Certainly nobody emerged into the chill morning from the café's interior, where those not obliviously earbudded were likely hunkered in routine annoyance against the saw's zip, much as they'd be for a passing siren or the clunk of a truck's axle in a pothole—nothing off the ordinary urban-decibel scale. The soap complainer had wandered away when Stevick wasn't looking.

The jackhammers, though, drew complaint. Several exasperated café denizens packed their laptops and muttered in the loose direction of the truck and its jumpsuited operatives as they fled the scene, like birds flitting to another treetop, and no more courageous. One of the café's counterpersons, a chubby guy in an apron, seeing business spooked, made a more forthright protest, even shaking his fist. But the small dimension of the task blunted his protest: By the time the jumpsuited pair had ignored the counterperson for a minute or two, minute smiles perhaps rippling their lips—or was this an effect of the device's vibration?—they were shifting the jackhammer back into the truck in favor of shovels and picks, with which they deftly cleared the hole of shattered black chunks. Stevick nodded consolation to the counterperson, who had, after all, poured his soapy coffee forty-five minutes ago. What remained of it was cold.

*

The excavation was complete by the time Stevick wandered by half an hour later, having picked up his dry cleaning from the Korean and used his own bathroom before circling back to the café. Rain still threatened, hadn't arrived. Stevick couldn't say why he was enthralled by the activities that had commenced with the truck's arrival; some intimation, he supposed in retrospect, though it wasn't uncommon for him to buzz the café two or three times in a procrastinating morning. The hole was steep and accurate, hewing to the spray-painted plan still visible in two corners where the lines of paint, meeting, had pooled and blurred: an inverted phone booth of emptied dirt and rubble. Three fat fitted planks lay stacked beside the hole, sized to make a rough cover, Stevick guessed. The hole's former contents had been heaped precariously at the curb—the hydrant wasn't likely to be back in commission too soon, at this rate. The orange cone remained, like an ill-fitted condom stuck on its head. The truck, however, was gone.

And then it was back, jerking to a halt at the curb before him, as if responsive to Stevick's own presence, to his attentions; however absurd this notion might be, Stevick had conceived it. With an unhurried persistence, the jumpsuited men emerged again and opened the van's rear, then stepped inside to wrangle out what at first might have seemed another object but then revealed itself to be a man, a human captive. The man was dressed in the same uniform, as though recently demoted from their company. But his skin, Stevick noted wearily, as if this fact beckoned to outrage he ought to feel rising within him but didn't, was darker than theirs. His head shaved, where their hair was intact; his two- or three-day beard rough, where theirs were, in one case, trimmed into a goatee and, in the other, shaved clean. So the jumpsuits, rather than suggesting equivalence between the three, framed difference. A cruddy cloth gagged the captive's mouth; another bound his wrists in front of him. His eyes didn't trouble to plead as his captors led him to the fresh hole and lowered him within, taking care not to scuff his elbows on the crumbled lip. They'd measured well: The captive nestled just underneath the three fat boards when these were fitted over his head. One of the jumpsuited operatives stood atop the boards, testing their firmness with apparent satisfaction, while the other quickly loaded the cones into the back of the truck. Now, at last, the rain began to fall.

"How—?" Stevick began, then faltered, unsure of his question. "How long are you going to leave him in there?"

The two could barely be bothered to hesitate, in their hurry for the shelter of the truck's cab. "We're on installation and delivery," the clean-shaven one said as he assumed the driver's seat. "Pickup's another department."

"Are we talking hours or days or weeks?" Stevick said, locating, perhaps belatedly, some faint civic courage, a notion that he'd absorbed certain duties as a local witness to the open-air procedure, perhaps by default, but no less legitimately for that. Besides, others inside the café might be watching through the window. His question was perhaps a feeble one, but for anyone observing, the fact that he'd stood up from the bench and begun some sort of stalling interrogation could be seen as crucial, either in a deeper intervention to be conducted by more effective or informed members of the community or in some later accounting of Stevick's comportment and behavior.

"I really didn't look at the schedule in this case," the driver said. "But they're rarely installed for more than three or four days in a single location."

"Anything longer wouldn't be seen as humane, I suppose?"

"More like these measures simply aren't effective beyond a certain point. Listen, we've got to go."

"Those boards are in no way tight enough to keep the rain from falling on him," Stevick pointed out. By placing their hole so near the hydrant, they'd prevented a parked car from giving shelter to the hole. On the other hand, perhaps they'd spared the hole's inhabitant something terrifying in being doubly pinned by the low ceiling of a vehicle's undercarriage. Probably Stevick was guilty of overthinking: It was impossible to find a parking space in this neighborhood, so they'd settled on the obvious solution.

"That's generous of you to notice, citizen," the driver said. He gestured to the occupant of the passenger seat, the goateed man, who'd been sitting with his arms crossed and rolling his eyes, miming impatience. Now this silent partner produced something from the floor of the truck's cab: a compact black umbrella—the inexpensive double-hinged kind you might purchase at a shoe-repair shop, having ducked in during a gale. He handed it to the driver, who passed it through the open window to Stevick. "This is why we're grateful you came along when you did," the driver said, nodding to indicate the hole. "Don't be afraid to stand on top—it'll easily support your weight."

With that they were gone, and for the last time. Stevick never saw them again; the driver hadn't been misleading him when he alluded to the narrow specialization of their tasks. Now there was only the hole, its occupant, and Stevick, with his own duties. For, when freed by the truck's departure he turned to face the café, no one in fact was regarding him from the window, now streaked with rain and curtained by a dripping overhang. Stevick opened the umbrella. The hole was silent. Stevick could easily have gone home, but instead he stepped over, tested the sound-ness of the footing on top—there was little doubt, he'd watched them work—and sheltered both himself and the sturdy boards from the rain as well as he could beneath the feeble rigging of black cloth and wire.

In a lull the aproned counterman stepped outside the café's doors for a cigarette break. He nodded curtly at Stevick, exhaled smoke rising into the rain. "So you're in charge now, huh?" he said.

"I didn't want to leave him completely alone." There had been no sound, barely a detectable motion from the hole beneath his feet, where the captive now sat braced, knees wedged in dirt. "I wouldn't say I'm in charge in any wider sense," Stevick continued. "I'm something of a stopgap or placeholder, really."

"I more than understand," the café employee said. "We're in a similar situation. Just a gig between real jobs, that's what I keep telling myself." He tossed his fuming butt into the gutter, quite near. "There's a million stories like yours and mine."

"That's not what I was getting at," Stevick began, but, uninterested, the counterman had returned inside. The café's population had never completely recovered from the jackhammer exodus; that, combined with the rain, kept Stevick's vigil a lonely one. He preferred it, actually. The usual early-afternoon dog-walkers passed by, hunched in tented plastic ponchos, their smaller dogs, the terriers and dachshunds, sheathed in sleeveless plaid coats, but Stevick had always regarded the walkers as ships on a distant sea, some passing flotilla. Even on days of bright sunshine, they were too occupied with canine herding and the management of plastic-bagged turds to engage in the human life of the street. Though few other humans acknowledged him, Stevick liked to believe that he was still a participant in this mainstream. Whether his relation to the man beneath the boards qualified as a human transaction was another question.

*

Toward evening, the rain tailed, though not enough so that Stevick lowered the umbrella. The café's clientele turned over; the tables were set for dinner, decorated with lit candles, menus in place; the staff even switched off the WiFi in order to chase out the most tenacious of the afternoon Googlers. Others of Stevick's neighbors, the professionally dressed, beleaguered rush-hour subwayers, slavers in financial offices, trudged past the corner with their own umbrellas. Though Stevick always thought of them as upright sheep, some were surprisingly bold in their muttering.

"What did you say?" Stevick shouted back.

"You heard me, friend. You're lowering property values for the rest of us."

"Not in my backyard, eh?" Stevick said. "Boy, when something like this arrives in your midst you learn pretty fast who's who in this neighborhood, you yuppie." Stevick spoiled for a fight, feeling now all the insurgent defiance he ought to have summoned for the diggers of the hole. But what was done, was done. Defense of what should never have been in the first place had become Stevick's province.

"You artists need to grow up and learn the difference between an installation piece and a hole in the ground," the man sneered. Surely Stevick's age or younger, yet dressed like Stevick's grandfather, he added, "Slack-ass."

Stevick was incensed. "There's a man in this hole!"

"Don't bore me with your disgusting personal situation!"

"It's not a personal situation, you fucker!"

"Roll up and die, grubbie!"

"*Yaaaaarrrr!*" They charged with umbrellas out-held, Stevick feeling he'd abandoned his station but unable to stem the urge to gore the man on the sidewalk and see him plead for mercy in the rain. Yet the two men essentially missed, failed to engage, the broad opened umbrellas merely grazing in a rubbery wet shudder as they passed. The single thrust having apparently exhausted his neighbor as much as it did Stevick, the man regathered his briefcase tightly beneath his elbow. "I need to go pay the nanny," he murmured as he slunk off. Stevick retreated to his task.

It was night, and inside the café the menus at several of the tables had been taken up, wine poured, little plates delivered by the time another specialist made contact with Stevick. He wasn't, as Stevick might have hoped, a sentry arriving to relieve Stevick of a duty that, now that he contemplated it, he had to admit was self-assigned. Rather, the jumpsuited man, a sturdy, almost fat one this time, with heavy, black-rimmed eyeglasses and a Yankees cap shielding him from the rain, appeared to be some kind of inspector, charged with ensuring the rightness of the site and recording in cryptic shorthand, with a ballpoint pen on a clipboarded sheet, certain impressions. The man double-parked his car, the blinking hazard lights of which gave clear evidence of the passing nature of his visit, and suggested to Stevick a long itinerary of random checks still ahead of him. He then politely asked Stevick for assistance in drawing aside the cover of planks. Stevick, in turn, extended the umbrella to help protect the operative's clipboard while he wrote.

The captive, Stevick noted with relief, didn't appear any more—or less—uncomfortable than when he'd first been lowered into his hole. He stood, as if to acknowledge the inspector's attentions, but didn't glance upward, possibly not wishing to incur rebuke, or perhaps he had merely grown incurious about what were, for him, routine operations. When the inspector went back to his car and returned bearing a wax-paper cup with a straw and a pair of plastic-wrapped sandwiches, Stevick understood that he intended to feed the man in the hole, and saw also that the captive had at some point spat the dirty cloth from his mouth, so that it now encircled his throat like a necklace. Probably it had never been secure to begin with, and the captive had not wished to embarrass the men who'd dug the hole by flaunting their ineffectual knotting skills. The inspector lowered both the cup with the straw and half a sandwich to within range of the captive's mouth, and the man in the hole quietly and efficiently fed and drank. Stevick considered the fact that the captive could have cried out at any point and had chosen not to. Perhaps he'd learned that it led only to more punishment, if punishment was the right word. Stevick had begun to realize that he ascribed a certain strength, a gravity and authenticity, to the man in the hole, or perhaps to the hole itself, with which he wished to be associated, as in the sense of a shared undertaking. The passerby with whom he'd crossed umbrellas had been, in a manner, right: This was a kind of personal situation.

Stevick helped the inspector replace the wooden planks over the hole, then gratefully accepted the gift of the second wrapped sandwich, which turned out to contain pleasantly peppery chicken salad, albeit on soggy white bread. Stevick had been hungrier than he realized. Before departing, the inspector went back to his car one last time, returning now with an olive-green duffel, which he chucked gently to the edge of the hole, just beside Stevick.

"What's that?"

"Standard issue," the inspector explained obscurely. "It'll be there when you need it." He offered Stevick a quick salute and was off.

*

It was only after the café had closed for the night, the chairs overturned on the tables, that the rain ceased completely, leaving Stevick with the question of whether his shift here ought to conclude. He shook out and shuttered the umbrella, and had just reached for the enigmatic duffel when he was greeted by the sound of his own name in the familiar voice of his ex, Charlotte. It was perhaps inevitable that she'd pass by if he camped out here all day. In another lifetime, which was what even yesterday seemed to be after this present occurrence, he might have been guilty of doing exactly that. As it happened, he'd overlooked completely the possibility of her wandering past. Charlotte was dressed and scented for a night on the town, clacking in her heels toward the subway entrance, most likely to undertake her usual carousel of Stevick's former favorite bars in the company of his lately-out-of-touch friends.

"Well, now, look at you," she joshed. "Keeping busy, as usual."

Stevick guiltily withdrew his hand from the duffel bag and stood alert to indicate his vigilance, though now, rain cleared, umbrella folded, it was hardly evident what his duties were. He'd always had to straighten his posture in Charlotte's presence, her height and perfect carriage a kind of warning or rebuke to him, and now he found himself wishing that she'd step off the curb, down to his level. The three planks that covered the hole were too expertly flush to the asphalt to be any help to him.

"There's a man in this hole, Charlotte." It was the second time he'd tried to even the field by stating this absolute truth, almost as if he needed to hear it himself to believe it, though he'd been presiding there all day. He wanted acknowledgment of his effort, but first he had to establish the basic situation.

"Sure," Charlotte said. "I've heard of this sort of thing."

"I guess I'd heard of it, too, though it's different to have it right in front of you. Still, I guess it has to be somewhere."

"True enough," Charlotte said. "I just hadn't pictured you getting involved. But by your logic, I suppose, someone had to step forward."

Stevick couldn't really improve on this sentiment, so he let it stand.

"So, what's in the bag?" Nothing was lost on Charlotte, he had to give her that.

"More sandwiches, I suspect," Stevick said, surprising himself with the guess. Should they be called rations, or provisions? It depended on who was eating them, he supposed. "They're not bad, if you like chicken salad. Take one, if you're hungry."

Charlotte had by this time poked inside the bag, assuming her usual privileges in regard to Stevick's boundaries, and pulled out a plastic-wrapped jumpsuit, identical, except for its virgin state, to those worn by the operatives and by the captive below. There appeared to be four or five of these stacked within the small duffel.

"You're hired!" Charlotte exclaimed. "You've been promoted from a temp position to staff."

Stevick found himself pleasingly able to ignore her goading. In many ways, Charlotte, like much else, was receding from view. The new conditions made irony a luxury. Was he meant to hoard the jumpsuits for his own use or to recruit other operatives from the neighborhood? Or, for that matter, were they intended for future incarcerees? Stevick considered the possibility that he'd eventually be fitted for a hole himself. The beauty of the uniform was that it settled nothing.

"Do you want to see him?" he asked Charlotte, and immediately regretted a question that seemed inappropriate, even somewhat craven on his part. He knew only after he'd said it that he would never again let himself use the man in the hole as a token or a bargaining chip. He was a person!

Charlotte's cavalier reply felt predestined. "No, thank you," she said. "I should go, I'm running late. But it's really good to see you doing so well, Stevick." Her voice was like a pat on a baby's downy skull.

The hint of tenderness cloaking Charlotte's dismissal disgusted Stevick. Talk about your passing connections! Stevick felt closer after a single day to the man in the hole, though they'd exchanged not a word. As he watched Charlotte make her way up the street, Stevick experienced only relief that she'd refused his suggestion. To pry up the planks when he had nothing to offer was a small indignity he had spared the captive below. The last thing Stevick wished to do, after all, was annoy him with inessentials. Success in an endeavor like this one lay in the details. Stevick was certain he was going to do a good job.

Their Back Pages

Page one, panel one, the island. A dense atoll in a wide barren sea peppered with shark's fins. Palm trees, sandy shore, pale lagoons, distant smoldering volcano, etc. Interior rain forest cloaking caves, freshwater springs, shrieking inhuman trills, a nest of ferns where bleached skeletons embrace, who can say what else.

Page one, panel two, the plane. A bolted turnip with wings, now aflame.

Page one, panel three, porthole windows of plane. In first class, the Dingbat Clan. Father Theophobe Dingbat, mother Keener Dingbat, son Spark Dingbat, daughter Lisa Dingbat. In coach, Large Silly (a clown), Poacher Junebug (a hunter), C. Phelps Northrup (a theater critic), Murkly Finger (a villain), Peter Rabbit (a rabbit), King Phnudge (King of the Phnudges), C'Krrrarn (a monster). Large Silly and C. Phelps Northrup are in black and white, all others are in color. All gaze downward, terrified, except C'Krrrarn, who plays computer solitaire.

Page one, panel four, splashdown. The plane's wings curl inward to cover its windshield as it crashes into the lagoon. The wings have fingers, and the doomed pilot and doomed copilot peer from between the fingers like eyeballs.

*

From *The Journals of C. Phelps Northrup*
July 14

On this fifth day of our desolitude I fear our little
compact of necessity has fractured. Mr. and Mrs.
Dingbat have refused Poacher Junebug's sagacious notion
that we depart the beach for the caves of the interior,
insisting that salvage is imminent and in trepidation
of the rumored wolverines and bandicoots roaming
the deeper groves. However, despite his intrepitude
and riflery, Poacher Junebug has succeeded in bagging
nothing, which circumstance neither allays our fears nor
stocks our larder. The hunter also continually alludes,
in snide asides, to the possible deluxe repast to be made
of Peter Rabbit. Hence, much dissension, resulting

in parturition of our ranks; Peter Rabbit now savors protection within the circled wagons of the Dingbat Family, on the sand where we first crawled ashore, while Poacher Junebug, Large Silly, King Phnudge, and I have undertaken to conquestify the interior. Murkly Finger has, too, stayed behind and entrenched on the beach, in a fragment of the airplane's darkened hull, within which he hoards untold provisions. Only King Phnudge has managed penetration of Finger's lair (King Phnudge has no arms and so perhaps represented no threat to Finger's cache), but his vocabulary was inadequate for conveying to us any sense of the inventory he'd espied there: "Creamy dreamy breamy—hip hurdle hoo!"

C'Krrrarn has of course from the first gone his own way. He was sighted again, by the brainy little Dingbat girl, early this morning, posed atop the volcano. Lisa summoned us all to see him there, still as sculpture, foreclaw beckoning to the new sun.

*

PRE-NOSTALGIA CLEARANCE SALE!!!
LIMITED EDITION DINGBAT SODA
REDUCED
FUTURE COLLECTOR'S ITEMS???
T. DINGBAT'S BEER COLA (nonalcoholic)
KEENER'S LITE ICE TEA
LISA DINGBAT'S CHERRY-ROOT BREW

SPARK'S FIZZUM (caffeine-reduced)
GONE BUT NOT FORGOTTEN???
TWENTY DOLLARS PER CASE
DINGBATS WE MISS U!!!

*

Ten-year-old Spark Dingbat wandered the beach at mid-day, wearing an inverted bowl of woven palm fronds, a sun hat fashioned by Keener, his mom. Spark had left his family and Peter Rabbit at the campsite they'd improvised, a ring of crappy lean-tos encircling a presumptive fire that his dad, Theophile, had serially failed to light. His sister, Lisa, having forged a twee, cooing alliance with the terri-fied hare, Spark was left somewhat on the outside. Now, obstinately solo, he strolled at the shell-strewn beach's exact margin, where the wiper blade of surf just dyed the pinkish sand a wetter hue, where his eight toes were teased by a fringe of bubbles.

Rounding the top of a rocky knoll, a view unfolded below of an inlet sheltered from the harder surf of the sur-rounding beaches. Two fat figures splashed there. Large Silly and King Phnudge. Spark clambered past the spit of rock and eased down the sand embankment, to stare from the inlet's grassy ridge. The clown had removed his shoes and clothing, all but his jet-black underwear. His feet were enormous, his white body both fleshy and firm, like the ripest fruit. King Phnudge remained fully dressed, or perhaps he was painted. His crown and beard seemed to flow into his collar, and his collar seemed to be one with his belt and his boots, less accoutrements than fancy outcroppings of his smooth, pudgy whole. Armless, he splashed excitedly side to side in water that came to what should have been his knees, while beside him the clown beat maniacally in the water with a large forked stick, a dowser who'd discovered the sea. The two made a natural pair in Spark's eyes. Their other strong resemblance was to his father, but Spark suspected no one among the islanders would ever remark it. His father was famous. Large Silly and King Phnudge were nobodies.

"What are you doing?"

Large Silly and King Phnudge wheeled, completely surprised.

"What's it look like, boy? Poacher said he saw some sea bream in this pool."

"Fishy splishy wishy hup huzzoo!"

"How are you going to catch them?"

"With nets of vapid questions and sarcasm. In our teeth. With that headgear of yours—hey, there's a notion. Cough up the fedora, lad."

"Use the king's crown."

"Crowns, if you hadn't noticed, have a hole in the middle. Besides, I don't think it comes off."

"Stuckity pluckity pizzazz—hooble hoo!"

Spark sighed and passed his hat to the eager clown, then watched as it was thrashed to fragments in the hope-

lessly clumsy attempt at fishing. Spark never saw evidence
of a fish. If there had been any, king and clown had certainly frightened them off. Keener's meticulously woven
palm fronds were borne off with the seaweed and foam in
the pool's gentle tide.

*

C'KRRRARN TEARS OFF THE TOP OF A PALM
TREE AND FEEDS!!!

C'Krrrarn is staying within himself.

C'KRRRARN TEARS OFF A CORNER OF THE
VOLCANO AND FEEDS!!!

C'Krrrarn is staying within himself.

C'KRRRARN TEARS OFF A CHUNK OF THE
OCEAN AND DEVOURS IT!!!

C'Krrrarn sits perfectly still and tries to empty his
mind.

C'KRRRARN SLURPS THE BLOOD OF THE
DINGBATS!!!

Long study has demonstrated to C'Krrrarn that the
other person is himself.

C'KRRRARN TEARS OFF A PORTION OF THE
HORIZON AND DEVOURS IT!!!

C'Krrrarn gazes into the horizon and the horizon
gazes into C'Krrrarn and each is calm and free of desire.

*

From *Poacher Junebug, an Index*

*

From *The Journals of C. Phelps Northrup*
July 27

Decline sets in. Tempests wreak havoc on our poor
dwellings every third day. Between, corrosive sunshine.
Despondent over prospects of rescue. We find little and
less to eat. Eighteen days and we come to know some
of our companions too well, others not at all. Murkly
Finger roams the shore at night, cackling. In sunlight

he retracts like a rodent to his hole, around which he has erected an array of sharpened sticks dug in pits of sand, disguised with flimsy leaf cover and more sand, and which would collapse inward at a footfall. The clown floats on his back in the spring where we would drink, moaning snatches of merry song, muttering wry punch lines without any jokes to them. He has forsaken his hygiene, enclothed in only his undergarment and a purple island hyacinth, its stem wended in his loopy tufts of hair. His feet are rotting. Poacher Junebug, I now understand, catches nothing, fulminates only. The rabbit is in no danger, except from himself. Like the derelict clown, the hare has abandoned clothing, shedding his red waistcoat and bow tie. He now goes on all fours, heeding some natural call. Lisa Dingbat, that former exemplary tot, follows him everywhere, and she too presently goes au naturel. I tried to confabulate with her one recent afternoon and she only sniffed and nibbled at the air, issuing a rabbity wheezing sigh, perhaps believing herself a sibling to Peter. The other Dingbats remain largely hidden from view. They must be hungry.

One seldom thinks of C'Krrrarn these days.

King Phnudge, unexpectedly, makes good companionship. We freqently embark on foraging walks together, gleaning nothing of consequence or edibility but nonetheless conveying if only to each other a heartening tone of decorum and kinship. King Phnudge alone, besides myself, retains the outward dressing of his former self (I should say: apart from my top hat, which was stolen and presumably devoured by a monkey). He cleaves to good cheer at all times and acts as though bounded, as we all once were, by the strict gutters and panels of decency. Despite his gormless patois, I find myself understanding his highness better and better.

*

Phnudgesong
    Fear and rage it shakes my soul
    I say only *Poorly Moorly—deedle dole!*
    I want to fuck and eat and strangle you
    I say only *Starving Carving—hoodle hoo!*
    Shit hole shit hole shit hole
    I'm sick of myself—*hup hizzole!*

*

"I'm better than this. I'm better than these people. I don't belong here!"

"Try this on, dear."

"I don't want to try anything on. I don't need another hat. I want my family, nobody's even listening to me. Where are the children?"

"It's not a hat. Lisa's playing with the rabbit, and Spark is out exploring the island."

"Quit crafting stuff out of palm fronds and frogskins and pond scum, Keener. Nobody needs that shit."

"Just see if it fits, Theo."

"How could they send me to a place with monsters and hunters and clowns and theater critics? The clown and the theater critic, they're not even in color and I want to go home! They make me feel old!"

"Nobody sent you, honey. Our plane crashed."

"It's a setup. It's always a setup. What were we even doing on a plane with those types? What is this, some kind of wicker hockey mask? I can't breath through this thing."

"Oh, that looks silly. It's not for your face. Put it down . . . there."

"You wove me a thatched codpiece?!?!?"

"I'm working on breastplates and a helmet. The samurai often wore wicker armor, you know."

"What good is wicker armor on an island?!?!"

"I'm just trying to get you prepared for a new life, lover."

"!@&$%#! I don't want a new life! I want my old life!"

"You'll eventually have to lead this island, Theo. Nobody else is going to do it. Peter Rabbit isn't going to do it. The black-and-white characters aren't suited for it. Poacher Junebug's discredited himself. King Phnudge, well, he's just not right. And Murkly is a villain."

"That's another thing, I don't want to go around there anymore, I don't like the way he looks at you!"

"He can't help himself, Theo. I just wanted to bring him a sun hat."

"Did he let you into his little hiding place?"

"Yes, we sat and had a very nice talk."

"I don't want you to have a very nice talk!!!!"

"Yes, dear. I won't in the future."

"How can I lead the island when I can't even keep tabs on the Dingbats?!?!?!"

*

Spark Dingbat ascended the volcano easily. It had steps. Near the top he passed a small pyramid of skulls in various shapes and sizes—a skull duck with giant ovoid eyes, a skull robot with antenna ears, a skull pig with a tiny bone beret incorporated into its cranium.

C'Krrrarn perched at the rim of the volcano, seeming bigger than he had in the plane, looming like an outcropping of the rock itself. As the tiny beret was to the pig's skull, so C'Krrrarn was to the volcano. Beyond C'Krrrarn, Spark saw trickles of steam seeping from between burnt-umber rocks, the undersides of which glowed orangely, like enormous briquettes. Seagulls massed on C'Krrrarn's brow and shoulders, their dried liquid droppings striping him in the manner of a jailbird character, perhaps some crow or weasel standing before a parole board of bulldogs.

"I hope I'm not bothering you."

C'Krrrarn did not speak.

"You didn't look like you were doing anything."

C'Krrrarn did not speak.

"Are you waiting for something?"

C'Krrrarn did not speak.

"My mom says you could just probably swim off this island any time you wanted, or else maybe walk along the ocean floor, but then where would you go, because it's not like you have a home somewhere, and maybe in a way this island is as much like a home as you've ever known, and maybe we even crashed here because you were sort of attracted to the island from the airplane, like you felt some kind of geomagnetic tropism or maybe you glanced down and it reminded you of your mom and dad, do you think that might be right?"

C'Krrrarn did not speak.

"Are you going to kill us all? Just kidding."

C.D.N.S.

"How can you sit like that in the same position for so long? Don't your legs or your butt fall asleep?"

C.D.N.S.

"My mom is weaving you a tatami mat out of all this crud from the beach. Do you know what a tatami mat is? She said you would."

C.D.N.S.

"Do you mind if I sit here for a minute?"

*

Note to artist: Everywhere along the bottom gutters of the pages now, muddy footprints, rabbit droppings, and Dingbat spoor (*ed.: What does that look like?*), forming an abject trail of smeary pictograms spelling out an unknown future.

*

Page forty-two, panel one, King Phnudge, alone in the woods. The island's sole monkey has approached him from underneath a fern. The monkey carries a hand-cranked music organ and wears a top hat. King Phnudge raises his eyebrows in delighted surprise.

Page forty-two, panel two, a campfire in a clearing. Large Silly and Poacher Junebug and King Phnudge and C. Phelps Northrup devour shreds of the monkey, whose scorched remains still hang from a spit over the fire. The monkey's carcass still clutches the organ. Northrup wears the top hat.

Page forty-two, panel three, in the brush at one side of the clearing, Peter Rabbit and Lisa Dingbat stared wide-eyed at clown, hunter, king, and critic as they eat the monkey. The rabbit and the girl are unseen by the others.

Page forty-two, panel four, moving on all fours, the rabbit and the girl silently slip into the woods, where they resume nibbling on ferns.

Page forty-two, panel five, night, the campfire, now abandoned by the others. Theophobe Dingbat tiptoes up to the extinguished fire, where he locates a charred monkey rib. He sucks at it thoughtfully.

Page forty-two, panel six, Murkly Finger. He crouches in his cavernous shard of airplane hull, reading a comic book, which is opened to a splash page showing C'Krrrarn towering over an alpine village.

*

From where he sat beside C'Krrrarn, Spark Dingbat could see into the island whole, as if he sat within a camera obscura. He saw his mother, now outfitting Poacher Junebug and King Phnudge and C. Phelps Northrup in thatched armor, adjusting the palm-frond breastplates over their torsos while they stood at awkward attention, trying not to disappoint.

He saw Large Silly covered in baked mud, with dried grasses stuck to his arms and legs, sitting beside the creek masturbating.

He saw his sister and the rabbit hiding in the grass watching Large Silly.

He saw his father standing on the beach angrily punching his agent's number into a wicker cell phone and listening for a signal.

As though with X-ray vision he saw, too, into Murkly Finger's lair. Murkly Finger sat surrounded by suitcases from the wrecked plane. Alongside the clothing Murkly Finger had laid out as a pallet on the ground was a neat row of reading materials. Among them was Spark's own collection of *Dingbat Family Cavalcade* and *Dingbat Collectibles Catalog.* Murkly Finger also had a set of limited-edition clothbound *Tennyson Trolley Sunday Pages,* taken from C. Phelps Northrup's luggage, a Dover paperback of *The Seventh Voyage of the Phnudges,* a copy of *The Oxford Treasury of Comic Strips,* and a stack of *HORRENDOUS TALES OF C'KRRRARN!,* issues number one through thirteen, sealed in plastic sleeves.

He saw the grave his sister and the rabbit had dug for the blackened skeleton of the monkey.

He saw the island's birds and bugs.

He saw himself, too, seated beside C'Krrrarn on the rim of the volcano.

Spark Dingbat saw the island whole.

*

Poem

Say, Keener Dingbat, I wrote you a poem
On a funny old island where much has gone wrong
Sit right back and you'll hear of my love
For your coiled scribbled hair and your spidery legs
Not so spidery though as the giant spider I killed
To protect you my love but should I have let it eat
Your husband and kids and that wretched vile clown?
Oh, Keener Dingbat, you're haunting my days
I seek you in the pale lagoon and at the hidden
      spring
I seek you like a sheriff hunting a walnut oh shit
I stole that line, I can't help myself, I steal everything,
      I am
Your Villain,
Murkly

*

From *The Journal of C. Phelps Northrup*
August 12

Rustling in our armor like a flock of pigeons
we stormed Murkly Finger's lair at dawn. We all
partookipated—I mean, all able-bodied adultish
manlike characters, even the dissolute clown, with the
sole exception of Theophobe Dingbat, who declined
command of our sally, leaving that to his spouse. The
scoundrel Finger proffered no resistance—rather,
welcomed us inside, so it was we at last unearthed his
secret: not the yearned-for stockpile of nourishing
provisions but the histories of our earlier selves, the
panels and pages of our lives precursive to banishment
on this island. Each of us retreated initially to various
corners of the island, to mull on that from which
we'd been distranded. Before he secreted it from my
meanderish eyes, I glimpsed a sample of the earliest
appearances of Poacher Junebug, in *Frontier Follies*—
once a much less squat and feral figure, Poacher at his
first flush had the stature and equipoise of a young Dan'l
Boone. And how King Phnudge must miss his Queen and
Phnudglings! I myself mourned an earlier self, the dapper
gadabout wit who'd mercilessly shuttered theatrical
kerfuffles with his encaustic pen.

By evening we'd received the first reports of the
clown's escape. It was the female Dingbat child who
alerted us, the first we'd heard her speak aloud in weeks.
We searched the isle from stem to stern but found no

sign of him. With Poacher I even ascended the terrifying volcano, where C'Krrrarn and Spark Dingbat keep their enigmatical watch. They refused our questions with resounding silence, but it was plain enough there was no sign of clown there, unless he'd disintegrated in the bubbling melt. It was not until the following morn that he reappeared, on the pebble beach, contentedly munching a word balloon.

Large Silly seemed happy enough to show us what he'd done: clambered backward into his own panels, using the gutters as rungs on a ladder into the past. A trick, the clown told us, that he'd learned from a duck. With practice, he implicated, we might learn it too.

*

Page eighty-eight, panel one, the cove. A large pile of antique black-and-white furniture from *Tennyson Trolley* is afire. Poacher Junebug and C. Phelps Northrup turn a spit on which five word balloons have been impaled. The edges of the balloons are gently browned. Junebug and Northrup both salivate greedily, their eyes like full moons.

*

def. *flotsam*: flot-sam *noun*
1. wreckage, debris, or refuse from another char-

acter's panels, found abandoned on the beach or floating in the water
See also jetsam

2. characters who live on the margins of cartoon lore, such as clowns, hunters, critics, monsters, children, or animals *(considered offensive in some contexts)*

def. *jetsam*: jet-sam *noun*

1. cargo or equipment that either sinks or is washed ashore after being thrown overboard to lighten the load of a cartoon in distress
See also flotsam

2. cartoons that have been discarded as useless or unwanted

*

"... and then, as shown on pages five through seven in issue forty-seven, Keener failed to make me a ham-and-egg breakfast in the manner to which I have become accustomed, on the morning before I was supposed to go onstage with the Rolling Stones, causing me to eat Pop-Tarts and therefore to completely fnargle the gig—hey, are you getting this down?!?!"

"Sorry, yes, if you could just go a little slower, Mr. Dingbat."

"I'm paying you twenty-five clamshells a day to take dictation on my memoirs, critic, not to surreptitiously nibble on those crispy word balloons you've got ineptly hidden in your palm-frond satchel!!"

"Most sorry, Mr. Dingbat, but you really should taste this one, Poacher acquired it in C'Krrrarn, issue number seven, *The Caverns of Despond,* it has something of the dank savor of a truffle mushroom—"

"Give me that!!! Mmmm, crunch, slurp, crunch, slurp . . ."

"Now, try this one, it was spoken by a fair lass from, ahem, my own adventures, and makes a perfect tonic, if I may be so bold, a counterpoint to the first . . . it has the bite and tangicity of a Vermont apple, perhaps a Pink Lady or a Red Delirious . . ."

"Ahhh, crunch, munch, glug, glug . . . ah, this is hopeless, we're never going to write my memoirs!!!"

*

From his place where he sat beside C'Krrrarn, Spark Dingbat saw his sister running in the woods with the rabbit. His sister had grown fur and a small tail.

From his place where he sat beside C'Krrrarn, Spark Dingbat saw his father swimming joyfully with the clown and the critic in the surf. Their three pudgy bodies resembled dolphins and it was hard to tell one from the other.

From his place where he sat beside C'Krrrarn, Spark Dingbat saw his mother in a tower she'd painstakingly constructed out of plywood made from the woven-together heat and stink and motion lines salvaged from the panels of the other characters. She was in the upper room of the tower, humping Murkly Finger, who still wore his cape and hood.

From his place where he sat beside C'Krrrarn, Spark Dingbat saw King Phnudge commanding his army of slave Phnudges as they carried his castle forward, brick by brick (bricks balanced on their miserable heads because they had no arms) and reassembled it on the far side of the island.

From his place where he sat beside C'Krrrarn, Spark Dingbat saw Poacher Junebug with his bamboo spear and his wicker sack full of word balloons, returning from another successful expedition.

From his place where he sat beside C'Krrrarn, Spark Dingbat saw Spark Dingbat in his place where he sat beside C'Krrrarn. They sat on two tatami mats, a large and a small, woven specially by Spark's mom. Each subsisted, for the time being, on thought balloons, which they swallowed as soon as they arose, without opening their mouths. It was enough.

The Porn Critic

Kromer couldn't operate hedonism but these days it operated him, in the way that a pinned cylinder operates a player piano. What he knew came mostly from books—Anaïs Nin, William S. Burroughs, *The Hite Report,* stuff gleaned as a teenager from his parents' shelves. Yet in his current circle of Manhattan friends, who were mostly graduate students and legal proofreaders, Kromer played the role of satyr. The more he protested that it was only a single heroin-laced cigarette that had happened to be placed in his hand, or that his so-called threesome had consisted of scarcely more than heavy petting and a brush with sleep apnea, the more they looked to Kromer as their saint of degeneracy.

Kromer's reputation had its origin in the parties he was dragged to by a former schoolmate: a raven-haired, baggy-eyed heiress named Greta. Though these parties were invariably disappointing, Greta invariably closed them down. When a host was reduced to switching off lights and hinting that the sofa wasn't available, Greta took Kromer on her finishing rounds, often in the rain. Kromer worked nights, so the hours didn't bother him, and he had nothing else to do. Greta's legacy, a large trust fund she wasn't permitted to touch until her thirtieth birthday, drove her mad with the determination to die squalorously before she became wealthy. "Hell, I've been in three kinds of threesome," she once told Kromer, her lips tremulous and her eyes fixed on some dreamy distance, in a way that made her look as if she were on the brink of tears or insane laughter, but in fact indicated that she hadn't slept for two or three days. "With two boys, with two girls, and with a couple. The only kind I can't ever be in is the kind I'd really like—three men."

Greta was, in her desultory way, the real thing. The difficulty was an uncooperative world, slouching through a new propriety under Clinton. Everyone else Greta knew had been molesting their trust funds since prep school. That was the problem—they were responsible to their money, while Greta waged war on hers. Her only privilege was the use of her father's "man," a do-anything emissary and delivery person, who always picked up the phone and, astonishingly, would deliver Corner Bistro hamburgers fresh and hot to any downtown dive bar, usually one occupied primarily by pre-op transsexuals, where Greta and Kromer might be hanging out. Greta sometimes needed to borrow the fifty cents to make the call. Kromer, once he'd learned the trick, urged Greta to use this service often, as it would generally put an evening out of its misery, bringing on the sleep Greta badly needed but resisted. Kromer assumed this deliveryman or fixer was really a butler, but the one time he referred to him as Jeeves, Greta seemed not to get it.

From Greta's many aspiring transsexual acquaintances Kromer remained terrified of accepting even a blow job. None of them could have guessed what aura they'd transferred to Kromer. The process was mysterious. A book nerd, a clerk, Kromer sat failing even to drink very much among young blacks in stuffed brassieres who the following day would be late for beauty school or, in some cases, Intro Soc or Psych at Queens College. Their special language—"shemale," "pre-op"—made them a nerd species, too, Kromer understood. Yet, the next day, attending afternoon breakfasts with his wondering cohort of PhD candidates and proofreaders, Kromer played the part of Rasputin or Gurdjieff, expected to launch foul seductions or even abductions. Perhaps this was a matter of sheer phrenology—the suggestion of something sallow and ominous in Kromer's jawline and eye sockets.

Renee and Luna, in History at the Graduate Center—Kromer's names for them were Beautiful Renee and Invisible Luna—practiced the buddy system, never letting themselves be caught alone with him. Kromer learned this fact from their bolder colleague Sarah, who was willing to meet Kromer unaccompanied in Union Square, at least by daylight. The afternoon was bright, pigeons combing mud baked by winter, a scarf keeping Sarah's mouth hidden. Kromer had been speculating that Sarah might want him herself, when she mentioned Renee and Luna's policy.

"They shouldn't be afraid of me."

"They're not afraid. They're dizzy and repulsed. They want to be able to compare notes."

Notes? Kromer was a hinge between worlds, a glimpser. All he had to offer them was his own notes, not the world itself. This situation he couldn't make understood.

Nor could Kromer confess that it was Renee, all-but-dissertation on contemporaneous Western representations of the Boxer Rebellion, whom he loved. Renee Liu, who wore turtlenecks and resembled a whippet, her nose a beacon of melancholy, who furrowed her brow and laughed in suspicion of anything Kromer said that was halfway sincere, whose older sister had been at college with Kromer and Greta, and whose tiny Chinese parents Kromer had once therefore seen picking up Renee's sister and her belongings at her dorm.

Kromer had no idea whether Renee knew this, or whether her sister had told her terrible stories about Kromer's college years. But he couldn't interrogate Sarah on the subject, for fear that she might be injured by being overlooked in favor of Renee. What Kromer wanted to injure was the image of himself as debauchery's emissary. He said nothing. They fled the frozen park for a coffee shop, where Kromer suggested hot chocolate, adding, he hoped, a brushstroke of harmlessness.

*

Was it Greta and her pre-ops, or the depth of Kromer's eye sockets? Kromer knew it was also his job, what he was a clerk at. The shop was called Sex Machines. There Kromer retailed chunky purple phalluses, vials of space-age lubricant, silver balls and beads for insertion, latex dolphins with oscillating beaks. The shop's owner was a maven of Second Avenue, a hedgehog-like, grubby genius of street-level commerce. The possessor of a block of storefronts, his specialty lay in preempting hipster entre-preneurship with his own fake-indigenous coffee shops, video-rental emporiums, and, finally, the erotic boutique.

Sex Machines' interior and stock had been painstak-ingly derived from that of a famous San Francisco shop, founded by a sex-positive lesbian collective. In lieu of such a collective, the owner had installed Kromer, transferred from the video-rental outlet, as both manager and night man. Night hours were what counted in this instance. A wizard salesman, Kromer switched on and demonstrated the range of speeds on any number of devices with a shame-dissolving forthrightness. At those moments, he thought of himself as a Conceptual Lesbian, a term he'd invented and never spoken aloud, nor advanced into any coherent definition. Kromer was fairly certain he'd never experienced an erection within the bounds of the shop.

Four things. Pre-ops, eye sockets, Sex Machines, and the state of Kromer's apartment. Few had been inside, but word evidently got around. Kromer's boss, whose video store featured "staff picks" shelves with extensive written remarks, had insisted that Sex Machines produce their own version of the San Francisco collective's newsletter, a hallmark of that store's unfurtive friendliness. In the newsletter, pornographic movies were extensively categorized according to predilections and interests, and rated on several indices: number of key scenes, story or its desirable absence, diversity of performer types, et cetera. It seemed that this was the way to sell porn to bored marrieds, a market Kromer's employer characterized as "Moby Dick."

Kromer, outed once in conversation as a novice writer, was deputized as the editor of the Sex Machines newsletter, as well as its sole contributor and reviewer of new materials. His apartment was a maze of stacked porn. The volume was staggering. The disarranged piles melded into a wallpaper of ludicrous fonts and slashes of pink, brown, and yellow flesh; though the job was chiefly a matter of inventorying characteristics, tabulating spurts and lashings, Kromer couldn't get through the tapes fast enough. As invisible to him as familiar bookshelves would be to another, the accumulation tended to make a powerful impression on visitors. This Kromer ought to keep in mind, but hadn't.

*

It should have been foremost, especially on that in-like-a-lamb evening in March, a month or so after his stroll with Sarah, when Kromer improbably pried Renee and Luna loose from a dull celebration held at a pub just a few blocks from his building (some underdog had passed his orals, on second attempt). Kromer had brought Greta along, and it was she who actually accomplished the trick, keening for Kromer to lead her back to his apartment, where she knew he had a fresh bag of good pot. "Do you want to get high?" Greta, inserting herself beside Kromer, posed this question flatly to Renee and Luna, whom she'd only just met. Greta's dress, mascara, and mannerisms in this company made her appear a woman garbed as a bat or a cat at a party where no one else was costumed. She was an instinctive corrupter and seducer, guilty of everything ever imputed to Kromer. Yet he'd never have carried off the extraction himself.

The walk couldn't have been improved, Luna falling in beside Greta, Renee lagging behind with Kromer, the air nearly balmy. Kromer peppered Renee with teasing questions, even dared express surprise at learning of her sister.

"We must have been at school together. If I tried, I'd remember her."

"Think of me but better looking. She was a model. Now she's a model's agent."

"Really?"

"Not the famous kind. In catalogs for winter gear, under hot lights. She told me you could lose ten pounds in one session, just mopping sweat."

"Like a starting pitcher, I've heard." He threw a pretend forkball.

"Completely demeaning work."

"I'm sure," he said, ignoring the ominous word, failing at that moment to worry about his association with the demeaning work of removing clothes under hot lights rather than piling them on. "You could be one."

This drew her furrowed laugh. "Look at this profile. I'm a pig, I'm a dog."

He held up an *L* of finger and thumb, making the shape of her regal or mournful nose, something he'd practiced alone, imagining fitting his hand to its length. "I'd cast it in gold." The line came from somewhere, surely, but wasn't practiced in the least. It startled not only Kromer but Renee, too, enough to spare him the laugh.

"I've been wanting to find a way to split you from Luna for so long I can't say," he told her. "This little distance of pavement is all I've managed."

Renee watched her feet, and Luna's and Greta's, ahead. "There's always the telephone."

"I'd heard you two had a party line—was I misinformed?" He hoped the joke wasn't too antique for her. Their knuckles brushed. Not quite fingers entangling. No one said ouch.

But the walk, that brief elbow of Houston and Ludlow, was done. Their appointment with his baggie of pot commanded they exit the sweet night, in favor of the radiator thud and hiss of his walk-up. The super hadn't yet adjusted the heat to the season, so Kromer balanced blazing pipes with yawning windows. Air so plush at sidewalk level would be like ice coursing through his fourth-story windows. He'd apologize for luring them into a sauna riven with blasts of cool, nothing else.

*

Did Renee glance at the tapes on the bracket shelves, and the tapes stacked in uneven piles on the floorboards beneath the shelves, and the tapes on the shelf above the closet's hangers, where Kromer put all their coats? Possibly. Kromer caught Invisible Luna's glances at them. Yet it was Renee's containment that Kromer should have taken as a sign. She fell silent, her limbs surrendering their animation. If only the blocks of Ludlow had each been a mile long. Greta sat cross-legged on Kromer's couch and rolled joints with the crafty intensity and patter of a stage magician, so practiced that she could look away from the trick to meet her audience's eyes.

"Is all this yours?" Luna said. "I've never seen anything like it."

Kromer seized the opportunity with relief. The tapes had first to be mentioned, so as to be dismissed. "I find it pretty incredible myself," he said. "My mansion of smut has many doors."

"What's that supposed to mean?" Luna said.

Kromer cut the jokes, opting for efficiency. He described the formulaic nature of the reviews, how he'd become adept enough to write one after slogging fifteen or twenty minutes into a given feature, and the logistical annoyance of the VHS cartons stacking up. "You'd never think they could need so much of it, until you see them in the shop, ravenous for new releases. As if watching the same one twice would be the shameful act." The pronoun "they" was what he meant to put across, a verbal quarantine on the unseen behaviors dividing customer from clerk.

For a few minutes, the subject went underground. The joint circled the room. Kromer was content to see that as it visited under Renee's elegant nose she sipped deeply, eyes closed. He couldn't have predicted that it would be a fuse on a stick of dynamite, a spark sizzling its way to Renee's lips. Or that she'd go off like Yosemite Sam. Kromer was just dropping the needle onto a Cowboy Junkies LP when Renee screeched, "I feel like I'm sitting inside a copy of *Guernica*!"

"Sorry?" Kromer said.

"I can't let my eyes rest anywhere," Renee said. "It's like a meat shop—carnage everywhere."

Greta's eyes widened, which put them at half-mast. "More like Francis Bacon," she murmured. Greta had been an art-history major at college. "Really, if you squint, it's like we're in a Bosch painting."

"The Garden of Earthly Delights," Kromer said. It

seemed a calming phrase to utter, akin to saying the words *The Peaceable Kingdom* or *Everything That Rises Must Converge,* or like the narcotic tone of the LP, which presently purred, "Heavenly wine and roses seem to whisper to me when you smile . . ."

"My gender-studies professor did a book of life histories of sex workers," Renee said. "But it'd take a thousand years to debrief this Aladdin's cave of contorted bodies." Renee's expression was mangled, like her words.

"If these walls could talk, they'd moan," Greta said.

"I think they might be screaming at me," Renee said.

"Not everything is . . . the same as everything else." Kromer recognized that his generalized protest against equivalences wasn't going to cut much ice. As it happened, a bookshelf at Sex Machines featured Renee's professor's book, a fact Kromer didn't feel obliged to mention.

Renee bolted upright, putting Kromer on alert for a police raid, or a blouse aflame from a loose ember. Instead she darted at the edifice of porn, coming away with three tapes. These she tossed into Kromer's lap, poisoned potatoes. "Tell us what's so different."

Where could he possibly begin? Kromer flashed on the tapes' contents, helplessly. Actually, Renee had done well, for a random stab. Two of these three had some redeeming imaginative elements. He lifted the topmost, *Bare Miss Apprehension.* "These—I mean, *Bare Miss Adventure* and all the sequels—they're really just star vehicles for Jocelyn Jeethers. A picaresque structure, but charming. People like them, I mean. There's a good focus on female autonomy—" Kromer stumbled on the proximity of this word to "anatomy."

"Autonomy of what?" Renee said.

"Autonomy . . . of pleasure, I guess." He felt himself whirling down his own motormouthed drain. "Whereas this—" Having shunted the first tape aside, he held the next, *Anal Requiem 4: The Assmaid's Tale,* exposed in his lap. He hesitated over the terms "low end" and "bottom drawer" before settling on "Junk."

"That's your whole review, O mighty critic?" Invisible Luna said. No one threw him a lifeline here.

"Oh, I tallied up the number of certain acts, which is all you're really dealing with in this case." He flipped it away. "This, on the other hand, is actually pretty interesting." The film, called *Social Hormones,* Kromer had stayed with to the end. "The Sward brothers are renowned for their commitment to establishing character arcs and narrative causality, and production values generally—you can actually watch their stuff more or less like a movie, if not a great one." He heard quotes from his own newsletter entry. "Of course, there's a certain ceiling on the quality of the acting." It struck him, too late, that he was attempting to demonstrate that he wasn't a man from the moon by detailing the moon's topology, cataloging its hollows.

"Let's watch it!" Greta said.

"Or not," Renee said. She looked ill. All glanced involuntarily at Kromer's large black television, stacked with the VCR on its rolling cart. "Is it just me," Renee continued, "or are the walls getting closer?"

The suggestion's power was tremendous. Kromer, though eager for a subject on which to agree with Renee, thought better of saying he'd noticed it, too. "I really should clear some of this out—"

"You could just brick up the windows," Luna mused. "It's like a Gothic nightmare, what's it called—*The Prisoner of the Rue Morgue*?"

"By Edgar Allan Porn!" Greta shrieked.

Renee jolted from her chair a second time, now veering to the room's shrinking center, avoiding the looming shelves. She pitched, bent double, attempting a vomity dash for Kromer's bathroom. She nearly made it. The vision she'd offered earlier—the pig, the dog—now came fully into view, though Kromer felt anything but unsympathetic. She brushed him off, after he'd gained a brief, delicious sensation of her long knobbed spine beneath his fingers, and staggered to the toilet to finish her heaves. Kromer's special literacy was, it now seemed, something worse than a complete dead loss on the human scoreboard. It was positively toxic, able to compel vomit from gorgeous women. He thought with relief how, on her knees, at least, Renee would be spared any view of the VHS tapes stacked on the porcelain tank.

Kromer labored at the floorboards with wadded paper towel and citrus solvent, wishing to spare her, too, the shame of her stinky action painting. He glanced over to see Luna and Greta side by side on the couch, charting his efforts with amusement, Greta's short fingers meandering on Luna's archer's-bow thigh. Behind him, the apartment door slammed.

*

The permanent mystery was how much you seemed to know before you knew anything at all. Or maybe the permanent mystery was how stupid you could be and yet how you clung to evidence that your stupidity knew things you didn't. Kromer, just for instance, had named her Invisible Luna without grasping that it was he, Kromer, who was invisible to Luna. She was, he saw now, a pining, tentative lesbian, in love with her best friend.

Kromer's Conceptual Lesbianism had come with no gaydar. He'd kept Luna blurred in his periphery not only as a defense against how little he signified but also for fear of understanding his small role: Arousing but creepy, Kromer could keep Renee in a state of prurient susceptibility, yet repulsed by the male prospect. For Kromer and Luna had shared the same quarry, she who'd puked and vamoosed. Kromer's pointless reputation had once again run his tender hopes into the dust. As for Luna's hopes, who knew? Kromer had overplayed his role, or his apartment had.

Likely neither had stood a chance with Renee. Of such stuff booby prizes are made. Invisible Luna's breasts, fully visible now in the streetlight glow leaking in through

Kromer's bedroom windows, were lovely to touch. Kromer
was left alone with them while Luna submitted herself to
Greta's actions, lower down. The air was mingled sweat
and smoke and vomit, the hour unknown. Needle bumping to the label, at groove's end again. It was all good, it
was fine, it was okay, though Kromer had missed dinner and felt hungry. For hours he'd been rising from the
futon to change the record, knowing he was the inessen-
tial factor, never certain he'd be welcomed back when he
returned. But the prospect of the exotic thing you'd recall
forever, the alluring taint of a sophistication you'd never
quite scrub off, kept Kromer's small place open for him,
so long as he knew better than to remove his pants. Now
he felt too lazy to change the record.

Kromer was once more a conduit, a proprietor. He
might as well have been at the counter of Sex Machines, his
life a site where others came to test their readiness for what
they feared were their disallowed yearnings. Whether that
left room enough for Kromer's own yearnings remained
unclear. In the meantime, Kromer was the kind of good
egg who'd do his best to make certain Luna never knew
what kind of threesome Greta truly wished she could sub-
mit to. No one would ever understand the little sensitivi-
ties that went into making Kromer's sort of sleazeball.

When Luna was gratified, exhausting herself on the
horizon of her own possibilities, she gathered up underwear and reassembled herself with a certain horror in her
eyes, then followed Renee's path and fled the apartment,
leaving Kromer and Greta alone together on the futon. It

was the sort of foggy finish they'd given to plenty of evenings, though never before minus Greta's outfit and parts of Kromer's. Greta, enemy of sleep, rolled another joint. Kromer put on another record, got back into bed. Greta unbuttoned his jeans.

"It's okay," Kromer said. Maybe this was what he and Greta had in common. As opposed to oblivious solid citizens like Luna, Greta was another good-egg sleazeball, who'd worry that Kromer hadn't gotten a release of his own.

"No," Greta said, trashing his theory. "I want a dick in me now."

Not Kromer's in particular; this was just Greta's characteristic honesty. Kromer felt he had a bargaining position, for once. "I demand Barney Greengrass. A whole smoked-fish plate, with plenty of bagels. Sable and sturgeon, and chopped liver, too. Call your dad's guy."

"They're not open—it's the middle of the night."

"They'll be open in an hour or two." He stilled her hand with his own. "Call the guy first, set it up. Coffee and orange juice, the whole thing."

Greta sighed, then picked up Kromer's phone and did as he'd asked. Then she took off his pants. Kromer thought, Now I've added prostitution to my roll call of glamorous crimes. *I fucked for sturgeon.* But no, that would be playing the game by their rules. Kromer knew better than ever his wearisome sacred truth, which no one, perhaps not even Greta, could see: He was innocent.

The Empty Room

Earliest memory: father tripping on strewn toys, hopping with toe outraged, mother's rolling eyes. For my father had toys himself. He once brought a traffic light home to our apartment on the thirty-somethingth floor of the tower on Columbus Avenue. The light, its taxi yellow gone matte from pendulum-years above some polluted intersection and crackled like a Ming vase's glaze where bolts had been overtightened and then eased, sat to one side of the coffee table it was meant to replace as soon as my father found an appropriate top. In fact, the traffic light would follow us up the Hudson to Darby, to the house with the empty room. There it never escaped the garage.

Another memory: My playmate Max's parents had borrowed, from mine, a spare set of china plates. I spent a lot of time visiting with Max and, when he let us inside his room, Max's older brother. So I was present the afternoon my father destroyed the china set. Max's family lived in a duplex, the basement and parlor floor of a brownstone, a palace of abundance . . . Max and his brother had separate rooms and a backyard. All this would pale beside the spaciousness of our Darby farmhouse. That was the point.

The return of the china had become a running joke between our two families, or at least for Max's parents. They kept trying to give it back, my father kept explaining that we really had no use for the second set; he claimed that it had been a gift, not a loan. In this my father struck them as facetious, when he was actually not only sincere but losing patience.

This day my father had swung by on his way home from Penn Station to pick me up. His work was taking him to Albany more often. While they stood in the kitchen, Max's father took him by surprise, placing the stack of scrupulously cleaned china into my father's free hands.

"You really don't want them?" my father confirmed, in his dry way.

"No, please," said Max's father.

"Well, then, we'll just do this," declared my father, opening his hands. The plates dropped and exploded, slivers finding every corner of the kitchen and the living room carpet beyond. There, memory halts. Max and I were reduced to pen pals when my family moved.

The New York State Department of Housing and Urban Development was my father's employer, and we went upstate to be closer to his work. The move, though, was sold to my sister and me as a kind of bodily impulse on my family's part, like that of salmon spawning, to reject the hectic, compromising city in favor of a place where we could live. I was old enough to fantasize about the teenagerish collections of who knows what I'd cunningly display in a bedroom of my own, and how I would exclude Charlotte and her friends, and then how, later, with great ostentation, I would allow them to enter.

The movers poured our belongings into the new home. Its hugeness, the endless closets, the fact of the barn and garage: These performed a magic trick on our stuff. My father's accumulations dwindled as if viewed through the wrong end of a telescope. Charlotte and I ran through the house in a fever, counting the doors, including closets, attics, cellar. We lost count at sixty. We then chose our rooms. One room was appointed a den, another a guest room. My father singled out a room downstairs, formerly the doctor's consulting office (my parents had purchased this house from the estate of a retired country optometrist), with one door and one window, otherwise a simple rectangle outlined with plain molding, and declared it the future site of the empty room. The room was empty now. So it would stay.

"What's it for?" asked his eleven-year-old son.

"Anything we want it to be," my father said.

"Can we play there?" asked his eight-year-old daughter.

"As long as you take your toys out with you when you're finished, yes."

He explained by means of a series of exclusions. I asked whether we could go inside and close the door. "There are no rules," he said. "But—" I began. "Except that it stay empty," he interrupted. "Can I eat in there?" I asked, a few days later. "There's nothing you can't do in there," my father said, mysteriously. "Our family eats together at the table," said my mother. Charlotte asked if it was my father's room. "It doesn't belong to any of us," he said. "It's just a part of the house. In the same way that Arfy lives with us but doesn't belong to us." On moving upstate we'd gained a puppy, to prove we had a backyard. "Is it Arfy's room?" asked Charlotte, perhaps misunderstanding. "Arfy, too, is free to use the empty room," said my father. "If Arfy poops in there, who has to clean it up?" I asked. We all glanced at my mother.

Then came a ritual cycle of first occupations, Barbies and G.I. Joes soberly scattered and collected under my father's gaze. My mother ignored it. One Saturday morning she slept in, and my father led us in to sit cross-legged for a breakfast picnic on the smooth, cold floorboards, our Pop-Tarts raised above our heads to keep them from Arfy's nipping bounds.

These episodes were grim and perfunctory. Mostly the empty room sat empty.

At summer's end Charlotte and I started at Darby's sprawling public school, an isolated compound encompassing a terrifying twelve grades. When we brought a new friend home, the room was glossed as a symptom of our in-progress expansion into the vast house, or as a "famous" oddness of my father's charm. Within a year, the empty room was a social asset, like my father's collection of comedy LPs or his back issues of *Playboy,* like my mother's attractiveness and her willingness to provide fresh-baked blondies during wintry *Gilligan's Island* and *I Dream of Jeannie* marathons. The empty room counted among the "cool" things imported from my urban existence, no matter that it was the symbolic opposite of that vanished life.

My father created a sign-in sheet at the empty room's door. My mother spent her afternoons managing it. This was the first thing she complained of when my father slogged in for dinner. If he arrived in time to personally hound kids from the room—always checking to make certain we'd faithfully emptied the space of baseball cards, Archie anthologies, Slim Jim wrappers, what have you—he'd honor us with an arched eyebrow and one of his verbal captions: "Multifarious Doings, I Presume" or "Goings-on, Unspecified, Ensued." Once, cigarette smoke was detected, the residue of a spontaneous radical act by my friend Mike's annoying friend Buzz, the empty room now the default hangout for a clan of Darby High boys I hadn't even particularly wanted to impress. My mother flushed us out, Mike and Buzz to their homes and me to my "real" room. When my father returned, she sent him in for a sniffing tour.

"This fails to pass muster at any number of levels," he began. "The empty room is like a living organ in our family's house." My father's interpretive monologues were getting arcane. We tuned him out before he'd finished articulating nuances of some new policy. "The lung could be seen to be the empty room of the human body, not mere negative space. By filling and emptying with the stuff of the world it stands as the most aspirational organ, in a literal sense." Charlotte, who had hoped to see me dramatically punished, quit the scene in an arm-flapping show of vexation. My mother wandered off.

Under the Reagan cuts, Hugh Carey's administration reluctantly disassembled HUD. In the months before my father was fired, my mother colonized the empty room, setting out on her great delayed project of transcribing the oral histories of our grandmother and seven great-aunts, whom she'd tape-recorded for her thesis in anthropology at Hunter. Charlotte and I ceded the room readily. We'd situated our lives elsewhere, mostly in the cars of our friends, or in the booths or parking lot of Darby's doughnut shop. My mother, wearing large headphones and operating her special tape player by treadle, labored on her project with an air of private fury like that of a sweatshop seamstress. But she never failed to remove her desk after each time she worked.

Months before I left for college my father quit driving to Albany every day. He'd been haunting the "corridors of power," in his words—more specifically the lunch counter of Allworthy's, the greasy spoon where the department had lunched and where some of his old colleagues now convened, mourning careers they'd taken for granted. Judging by the haul amassing in the attic rooms and garage, and the gilt-framed Hudson River School knock-offs cluttering the walls of the living room, he'd begun scouring the capital's dusty junk shops.

He brought little inside the empty room itself. A Penguin Graham Greene, a saucer stacked with five or six Oreos, a vintage transistor radio with a miraculous knack for receiving Bob Murphy and Lindsey Nelson's Mets broadcasts all the way from New York, albeit wreathed in crispy static. For a brief, angry spell it was my parents who reactivated the sign-in system, vying over the clipboard at the door, my father's original hand-ruled grid now a grainy blur in umpteenth-generation photocopies. When his claim on the room ultimately trumped my mother's, she set up an office in the guest room upstairs.

I registered this in passing. After I left for freshman orientation I made short work of whichever parent answered the phone, then asked them to pass the receiver Charlotte's way. The extra length of cord my mother had installed meant that the wall-mounted kitchen phone could be stretched, barely, to slide under the closed door of the empty room. I heard Arfy whining and scratching at the door.

"It isn't the fact that he's always in here," she said. "Or that half the time she's upstairs in her pedal-operated time machine. It isn't even that they never speak a word to each other. It's that every time either one tries to tell me what to do they start with 'your mother and I feel' or 'your father and I want you to understand' or some other stupid fucking bullshit that makes me want to puke."

I convinced them to pack Charlotte off on a Trailways bus to visit me during fall break, claiming we'd be treated to Thanksgiving dinner at a Northampton hotel by my girlfriend Deanna's family. In fact, Deanna and Charlotte and I spent that week scuffling around the vacant dorm corridors, eating fast food and ramen, listening to R.E.M.'s *Murmur* and smoking marijuana morning, noon, and night. Deanna was the first person I'd met who smoked marijuana like it was cigarettes; she was the first person I'd met who did a lot of things. I'd been certain she and Charlotte would get along. I felt my first pang of jealousy at the bus station, just moments after Charlotte pulled her duffel from the undercarriage.

"So you're the fun one," said Deanna, putting her hand into Charlotte's hair and mussing it upward into a tangle. "No wonder your brother likes me."

"I can think of a bunch of reasons he'd like you."

"You wanna let me do something about that hair?" Deanna mimed scissors. Charlotte widened her eyes.

On Thanksgiving Day the three of us took psilocybin mushrooms and sprawled on a dirty, marijuana seed–infested section of carpet in the middle of Deanna's floor. Occupying Deanna's dorm room for the drug trip, while the rest of the universe, so far as we knew, enacted a normative Rockwellian Thanksgiving, recalled my father's notions of the suspension of ordinary life within the bounds of the empty room. But Charlotte and I didn't speak of this. For dinner we'd bought cans of Chef Boyardee ravioli, just for the squalor, but felt no particular appetite. At four in the morning our flaming synapses crumbled in flames and we sagged on the carpet into cat-like slumber.

Charlotte failed to hide her tears at the bus station. For a few weeks more, before the fatal New Year's visit, I could flatter myself that my parents' world was a place both immutable and dull, a snow globe I'd been lucky enough to escape, and which remained Charlotte's misfortune to endure. I was the one engaged in chrysalid transformations. These made early December seem as remote from September, when I'd first met Deanna, as Darby's mileage from the moon. What right did my parents have to do anything but stand stock-still for my barely attentive scorn?

When I called to say I'd be spending Christmas with Deanna (we would visit New York this time) my mother sobbed. The women of my family were on a crying jag. "Well, you can't have Charlotte this time," my mother said, astonishing me. I heard my sister in the background, saying, "Let me talk, Zoe." Charlotte had begun calling them by their first names around the time our father got fired. I still said Mom and Dad.

"You have to come back," said Charlotte. Her voice was cold. "No," I heard her say, with the mouthpiece covered. "No, he can't have the phone, I don't care. Tell him to come out if he wants the phone."

"What's going on?" I asked.

"Rupert wants to talk to you." My mother's birdlike cheeping evaporated from the background.

"What's taking him so long?"

"He's getting dressed."

My father got on the line. "Okay, college boy, I've been deputized to insist you give us a gander at this lady of yours. I've heard good things, but I'd like to see the new paradigm assert itself under my own roof." His flippant mode was even more ponderous than his ponderous mode. I promised we'd arrive in time for New Year's Eve. My sister called from the parking lot of Darby Donuts the next day, to tell me: Rupert had implemented a new policy of shedding clothes at the empty room's threshold. Zoe had detected a corroded dribble down the clapboard outside the empty room's window: urine.

I'd called from New York on Christmas Day, then treated my parents to radio silence. They believed we'd be traveling up from New York City, but Deanna and I had closed ourselves again in the quieted dorms, needing nothing but our versatile bodies. When the last day of December brought a snowstorm, we set out hitchhiking on Route 9 at one in the afternoon—early enough, we thought. But rides grew scarce in the whiteout, and the sky was dark by three thirty, our feet frozen from trudging with our rucksacks out of the centers of villages, seeking an acceptable spot to begin thumbing again. To get warm we quit for a while in Pittsfield and spent the last of Deanna's parents' money on dinner, open-faced roast beef sandwiches au jus, at a place called Dewey's. I couldn't know if my parents understood how long ago I'd run through the funds for my daily needs at college.

Deanna and I began working the diner's parking lot, petitioning drivers there to spare us the open road. Within an hour, though it felt much longer, we found a merciful soul, a middle-aged man in a bow tie and hunter's cap, to drive us into Darby, three across in his pickup's cab, our bags, already drenched, bungeed in the back. Shame sealed our lips, the journey home a surreal plunge through a cyclone of white, sound-tracked by radio hymns.

Neither Deanna nor I wore a watch, but the Samaritan's dashboard said it was twenty before twelve as we disembarked. Was this a plan? No, it never was. Some unplans are destined to be remembered as if they were conspiracies. My father must, at the sight of the headlights in our driveway, have rushed from the empty room and begun dressing in the hallway. He stood in the corridor buttoning his cuffs when Deanna and I stomped out of the mudroom, through the kitchen door.

"Happy New Year, revelers!" said my father. Arfy clung to my leg.

"Where's Charlotte?" I asked.

My mother perched on the staircase. "When you didn't show up she called some friends," she said. Then, "How do you do, I'm the mother." Deanna went far enough up the stairs to take my mother's hand and bow. I said, "Well, we did show up!" trying to meet my father's exuberant tone, and failing.

"Your sneakers are soaked," my mother said. This was true of both of us; Deanna plumped down beside her rucksack to pry them off, though she had difficulty even undoing the laces. "Actually, everything's soaked," I said. Our jeans hadn't dried despite the Samaritan's blasts of engine fumes. "You feel like throwing this crap in the dryer?"

My parents fell silent. "Let me show you the world-famous empty room," I said, and, before my father could speak, added, "No clothes allowed." Deanna shrugged and began peeling away her outer layers. My girlfriend was a specialist in rising to occasions.

"It's almost midnight," my father whined.

"Will you bring us some blankets and pillows and stuff?" My father lifted a cookie from a desultory plate that had been set out, possibly many hours ago, and began gnawing. He could as well have chewed his shirtsleeve or arm.

Was my mother a conspirator, too? All I know is she executed my commands (for they really were commands) with robotic precision. She delivered pillows, copious smoothly folded sheets, and the guest bed's duvet to the door of the empty room. By this point Deanna and I were concealed naked behind it, having widened the gap only a few inches in order to toss our undergarments onto the pile. Midnight came and went unremarked on either side of that barrier. "Candles," I answered, when, as I opened the door to gather in offerings, my mother asked whether there was anything more we needed.

"Your parents seem pretty great," Deanna said with superb neutrality, as she lit the first of the joints she'd rolled. We'd switched off the empty room's ugly overhead, and outside the snow, dribbling down through a windless sky, glowed like blue cotton candy in the penumbra of the driveway's single bulb. We fucked twice, quietly but concealing nothing, Deanna's three outcries rising through the ceiling and floorboards above, Arfy curling meekly onto a pillow in the corner once it was clear no attention was available for her.

Afterward I crept out. My mother and father had retreated upstairs. Deanna and I used the bathroom and then I collected some Tupperware for future such occasions. I also gathered food, including a Saran Wrapped platter I found in the fridge, full of triangular sandwiches: chicken salad, cream cheese and cucumber, crustless and heavily salt-and-peppered, just the way we liked them. I moved the den's stereo into the empty room, too. It wasn't good, but good enough for Deanna's homemade cassettes.

Charlotte came tapping at our window, clued in by our tread marks in the snow or the flickering candlelight. Wrapping myself in a sheet, I raised the sash. Arfy keened delight, nosing at the opened window, and Charlotte waved off whatever friend had delivered her home. Headlights swerved into the night.

"What time is it, anyway?" I asked her.

Charlotte shrugged. "Four, five, beats me. Is that pee-pee?" She meant the yellow fling pattern staining the snow behind her. I nodded. "Sick," she said approvingly.

"Climb in."

The empty room, being a tabula rasa, bore aspects of total corruptibility, a potential we'd in childish obedience overlooked until now. Our poses, cross-legged in sheets around the plate of triangular sandwiches, the ashtray, and the flickering candle, which illuminated the tumble of pillows and duvet like a pink-pale mountain range, evoked perhaps a Native American or Haitian voodoo ritual site. Nothing of this scene would have signified much in a dorm room. Here: revolution.

"What's that?" asked Charlotte.

Deanna understood the question. "They're called Echo and the Bunnymen. This is 'The Killing Moon.' It's pretty much their best song."

"You got Mom's sandwiches? That's crazy." Charlotte accepted the joint from Deanna's hand. Arfy clambered into her lap.

"It's safe out there, if you want something from your room."

"You guys want to fool around, huh? Dream on, unless you want to put up some kind of tent out of these sheets. Because no way am I leaving here before you."

"You don't have to leave," said Deanna. "We already fooled around."

My sister raised her hand. "Enough about that."

"They're upstairs," I said.

"Well, congratulations on a unique accomplishment," said Charlotte, with sardonic emphasis derived from my father's manner, however much she'd have hated to believe it. "They haven't been upstairs at the same time in a year."

"If we keep the music playing I doubt you have to worry about them coming down."

"What are you suggesting?"

I gestured at the empty room, a vacuum laboratory.

"Haven't you ever wondered," I asked my sister then, "how much stuff we could fit in here, if we tried?"

The Dreaming Jaw,
The Salivating Ear

I do not think I shall visit my blog anymore. It is not so much the smell that discourages me—gulls have skeletonized the corpse in the entranceway, and the lapping tide has salt-rinsed the floorboards where the intruder's blood was once caked as thick as fruit-leather—as it is a certain malodor of memory persisting there. The stink of my disappointment being that stink which the sea's salt can never rinse.

*

I study my blog through binoculars from the distance of the boardwalk, but never approach. Gulls wheel over my blog's entranceway, vultures at my kill, much as they do above the splintery planks of the boardwalk, scavenging the greasy paper sleeves containing, if a gull should be lucky, some remaining tidbits of cakey frankfurter bun, the last dark rejected french fry like a withered witch's finger. Let anyone imagine I gaze at the horizon. It is a kind of horizon at which I gaze, an inner-made-outer vanishing point, a place where feeling ventures out to make a meeting with language and finds itself savaged.

*

I will not forgive The Whom. He would not forgive me.

*

I thought I would see justiny at last, but the tiny bird has flown. The question I cannot allow myself to ask: Were they not two, but one? Was The Whom pretending to be justiny? Or was justiny pretending to be The Whom?

*

It was him I killed. He is not unnamed. He has a name, even if inadequate, bogus, contrived. The man I killed, The Whom. It was The Whom who tried to enter my blog and it was The Whom I wanted to keep out and The Whom I laid low with a single remorseless thrust with the blunt editorial object I had carried with me hidden on my person and with which, gripped knuckle-tight, I lay in wait inside the entranceway of my blog. It was The Whom I wanted to reduce to gibberish with my disemvoweler, it was him I wished to see undone and unspeeched it was him who poisoned the well and stole the goose it was him who could never would never be silent I tell you it was never other than The Whom.

*

A man tried to enter my blog. I killed him at the entrance there. In order to make you understand I would have to go back to the beginning and that is impossible. I am not trying to hide anything, I swear this.

*

I could never have protected anyone. I don't know who or what I was trying to protect. Since the day I killed the unnamed man there has been no one else remotely near the blog, no evidence of justiny, not an extinguished sasparilla candle, not an herbal-cough-drop wrapper. justiny has gone, if he or she ever dwelled here. justiny, I now believe, was as frightened of me as he/she was of that malignant other, the man I killed. And will I go unpunished? I have come to believe so. My blog is a site on no map, is sanctioned in no precinct, patrolled by no militia.

Its occupants have only ever constituted its sole authority. The three of us, if it ever was three. Or two. Now gone.

*

A man tried to enter my blog last night. I killed him in the entranceway with a blow to the head. I felt in the impact as I heaved my cudgel and met with his grunting pumpkin-thick skull that he was dead, and I discarded the brain-oiled implement in the darkness there and ran upstairs and hid in a far high corner of my blog in bereavement and horror not so much at what I had done to the man I killed, to that rotting gourd full of evil, but at what I had done to myself and to my solitary majestic kingdom here, to my elegant elaborate and irreplaceable redoubt now beshitted in revenger's shame. But it was done. He is silent now. I will need to pass his body there in the entranceway if I am to leave, the mouth-stilled black form slumped in the dark joint of wall and floorboard with its dumb black legs blocking the threshold. I am not afraid.

*

I wait in the dark huddled like an animal now, but it is an animal I have come here to meet, an animal I am seeking to purge and correct, and to do so I have had to turn myself into an animal too. The time for tender thoughts is adjourned.

HA JAW IF YOU COULD SEE WHAT I SAW
WHEN I GLANCE IN YOUR VICINITY
YOU'D FUCK OFF TO INFINITY
YOUR EVERLOVIN' WHOM

*

What is going on here jaw I am so scared and freaked out this isn't funny any more why is the whom doing what he is doing and is he even who he says he is???? There r times when I cant trust anyone or anything even myself justiny

*

I've secreted myself in one of the upper rooms. I hold in my hand an implement, an editor's tool, the exact weight and shape of my indignation at the doings of The Whom. My blog must not be spoiled. I will defend it, I will defend it with my life. I need look no further for a cause than dear little justiny, of whom I see no sign. I suspect the poor creature has pocketed her- or himself in a cupboard somewhere, nibbling on stale crackers or fingernails with teeth chattering in fear of The Whom's depredations, to reemerge only when the foulness has been purged. The quarters of my blog must be made safe for those who've come for solace here.

*

O jaw u should of seen it when u weren't around he was dominating this place just screwing with everyones minds pretending he was u and sayin if im the jaw u r my bubble gum u r my popcorn u r the gunk in my back molars and u ought to wait im gonna floss u out eccchhhh gross jaw hes such a lowbrow cant u do sumthing signed desperately yrs justiny

*

More ruined rooms, unbearable even to specify in this log—so many of them now, chambers of my soul forever sealed against the night.

*

I built too near the sea. The salt air corrodes the inlaid rosewood veneer. And at the moon's perigee the tide licks my door. On some nights I sit in the parlor of my sad savaged blog and think it was only a dress rehearsal, a dry run. That I will build another blog elsewhere and make its seams tighter, armor it and therefore myself better for the world. But to abandon this one now would be to betray justiny. I say this to myself even as I hear the waves crashing nearer than I ever wished them to, the waves that are like a pulse of hatred beating in my forebrain.

MISS JAW I FIND YOU
ELEPHANTINE IN ALL REGARDS

WHY NOT JUST BUMBLE OFF TO THE BONEYARD
THE HONORABLE WHOM

*

We coexist, invisible to one another, an uneasy blind roun-delay within the forgiving architecture of my blog. Here, I find evidence of justiny's self-effacing encampments: squeezed-out tea bag neatly wrapped in a paper napkin, glass bearing a wilted daisy, scattering of dandruff, faint odor of lemon verbena or chamomile. There, I wander dismayed into rooms Whomed: overturned or demolished in derision, furnishings all glued upside down on the ceiling as in sophomore japery, library volumes with their pages torn or twisted from their spines, a turd curled in an ashtray. Once, I found a parlor cleared of all its treasures and bric-a-brac, which had been replaced with paper slips, fluttering on the floor like fortune-cookie fortunes, each bearing the name of one of the vanished items: wicker love seat, brass birdcage, croquet set, and so forth. I conduct my rounds in mournful diligence, reordering what can be reordered, sealing off quadrants when I must. At certain times I persuade myself an admirable stasis is attained: My blog abides, adapts, is made worldly by its users. At other moments I feel we three stalk one another: prey and predator that have each come under my roof, my own role unknown as yet. It is then I think I hear the blog ticking like a bomb.

*

O jaw dont ever leave us again like that u scared me so bad im shaking all over the place cant u see you've got responsive abilities now especially 2 me yr number 1 fan justiny

*

I decided I ought to take a week away from my blog, to absent myself from the site of creation, therefore to allow the inhabitants dwelling there to regulate themselves. It is an egalitarian space I have made, with its own social ecologies, and it would right itself, I was certain. When I returned I found someone had set ablaze the guest book, as well as the burnished ebony Bible stand on which the guest book had stood. The blaze singed the plaster scroll-work ceiling, soot and ash from the pyre forming a kind of rude tombstone or epitaph to itself, like the remains of a Klansman's torched cross or the horrendous skeleton of a lynching tree. I hadn't the heart to repair the damage to it and instead sealed the alcove where the guest book and Bible stand had been placed, and now though the blog has innumerable rooms and no one would miss one little nook or alcove, I feel it as a missing limb, a deletion imposed on me by forces malign, a first mortal blow.

MISS JAW YOU GOT A LOTTA ADMIRERS BUT FOR MY MONEY YOU JUMPED THE SHARK

BEFORE THERE WAS A SHARK TO JUMP
GO BLINK IN A BLIZZARD
AND MAKE LOVE TO A LIZARD
THE WHOM

*

Dear jaw be strong you cant let the haters get you down yr blog is a very fine blog with two cats in the yard now everything is easy cuz of u also try imagining a place where its always safe and warm come in you said ill give you shelter from the storm xo justiny

*

A descreator, a desecraptor, a desacritter—why such difficlutties spelling the word?—has violated the hallowed corridors of my sanctum. I found his words slathered in dripping red bold graffitist's capitals unscrubbable across the raw terra-cotta tile:

MISS JAW
WORMS SUCK EYEHOLES
YOU SUCK GUMBALLS
THE WHOM

I'll content myself imagining such a soul writhing under its own torments, and not give the defamer even the honor of my rebuke. He'll have moved on, I assure myself of this. Shambled off to pick on something his own low size. Still, I see his little haiku as if neon-imprinted on my eyelids' interior when I shut my eyes to sleep.

*

Someday the world will build a highway with an overpass leading to a cloverleaf feeding to an off-ramp to a parking area that will be full of tourist buses full of visitors hungering in anticipation, there to join the multitudes tramping hour after hour clutching snack-bar goodies as they marvel through the corridors of my blog, then to reboard amid the waves of satisfied oglers clutching geegaws, key chains and can openers and T-shirts from the gift shop adjacent to the restrooms near the parking lot of my blog, but until that day comes I hear the steady pulse and recoil of the sea and see the moonlight through the skylight and reflected off the polished banisters and I know that if it is only justiny, whether she or he is alone or stands for secret lurking others now or in the future, I have made it and it is good.

*

A first appreciation has come. A tentative thing, a shred of sensibility, something that tiptoed in on little cat feet and graced me with praise. A he or she, I can't tell from the byline: justiny. *I wuvvv your blog,* justiny said in a note, a seashell-pink crayon scribble on a fragile curl of tissue, the equivalent of a whisper, a thing I found stuck to my boot as I made my proprietary rounds, polishing brass railings and marble doorknobs and suchlike, and which I might so easily have failed to notice. I had a moment's impulse to whisper back: My blog loves you too, justiny, in its way. But I think my blog's love is more cosmic or Buddhist, more impassive and impersonal, than to need always to answer. My blog is for all ears that might listen, and who knows how many that might be? justiny happens to have piped up. (Barely.)

*

Though I promise myself I'll be patient, I find myself visiting my blog ten or twelve times a day, tracing with my echoing footsteps the boundaries of its magnificence, wondering when I'll know—or if I'll know—when another sensibility has sensed its noble call, the siren or lighthouse of my mind beckoning to theirs, and come to the doorway of my blog, entered and roamed and learned that they are not alone out here on the fringe of the real but that others have come before them and blogged so that they might feel less lonely. But I myself am not lonely. It is enough to have my blog.

*

I Sing My Blog Electric!
    I made my blog in the shape of a tesseract.

I made a blog and it is good.

A small blog, of clay and wattles made. Nine bean rows will I have there, a hive for the honeybee, and I shall have some peace there, for peace comes dropping slow, and I will hear the ocean water lapping with low sounds around the pilings, while I stand in the foyer of my blog, within the exoskeleton of its architecture, feeling myself to be its deep heart's core.

My blog is as big and small as my desiring.

I tried counting my blog's rooms and found myself retracing my steps.

It has many doors and yet there is only one way to enter it.

I tried painting my blog in oils and ran out of canvas.

I shall follow mine blog wherever mine blog shall lead.

I offer this, my blog, to the world, but I do not require the world to need it or accept it, for it is my very very own blog.

*

I made my blog strong, I made it with my hands, fitted the joists and the beams and the floorboards neat, planed the crooked surfaces, sanded the knots where there were knots and varnished the sanded knots until a blind man couldn't tell you their location. It was a fine labor of many days and it stands, my blog, by the salty beseeching sea, a stone's throw from where the searching tidal claws at their highest point mark the sand. My blog is an outpost on forever.

*

I have had a lovely inspiration: a blog at the ocean's edge, a blog-by-the-sea. I think I shall call it *The Dreaming Jaw, The Salivating Ear*!

Pending Vegan

Paul Espeseth, who was no longer taking the antidepressant Celexa, braced himself for a cataclysm at SeaWorld. He wondered only what form cataclysm would take. Espeseth had tried to veto this trip, making his case to his wife with a paraphrase of a cable-television exposé of the ocean theme park, one that neither he nor his wife had seen. Instead, his wife had performed judo on his argument, saying, "The girls should see these things they love before they vanish from the earth entirely."

So here he was. The first step, it seemed, involved flamingos. After he had hustled his four-year-old twins through the turnstiles and past the souvenirs, the stuffed-animal versions of the species they'd come to confront in fleshly actuality, his family followed the park's contours and were met with the birds. Their red-black cipher heads bobbed on pink, tight-feathered stalks, floating above the heads of a crowd of fresh entrants.

"Wait your turn, girls," his wife said. Yet, seeing that no turns were being taken, Espeseth led Chloe and Deirdre by the hands and together they jostled forward into the mob to find a vantage on the birds. His wife stayed back, tending the double stroller draped with their junk. Closer, Espeseth saw that the birds were trapped on an island, a neat-mowed mound of grass ringed with a small fence and signs saying PLEASE DO NOT FEED.

"Can you see them?" he stage-whispered down at the girls, as if the clump of exotic birds were something wild spotted in the distance, a flock that could bolt and depart. In reality, they'd had some crucial feather clipped, rendering them flightless, the equivalent of crippling an opponent in a fight by slicing his Achilles tendon. The birds had no prospect of retreat from the barrage of screaming families pushing their youngest near enough for a cell-phone pic.

"I'm scared," Deirdre said.

"They're scared, too," he told her. *As am I.* The flamingos were the first thing for which nothing could have prepared him. Having already watched with his girls a hundred YouTube videos of orcas, having already scissored magazine pictures of orcas and cuddled his children to sleep in beds full of stuffed orcas, Paul Espeseth had hardened his soul in readiness for orcas—their muscular poignancy, their mute drama, the chance that they might in full view and to a sound track of inspirational music disarticulate one of their neoprene-suited trainers at the elbow or the neck. But the designers of the park had outsmarted him, softened him up with flamingos, like a casual round of cigarette burns to the rib cage preceding a waterboarding.

The girls found their boldness and pushed up to the front, then relented, and were supplanted in turn by other eager, deprived children, presenting their faces in what he imagined was for the birds a wave of florid psychosis. In the context of their species, these flamingos were like space voyagers, those who'd return with tales beyond telling. Except that they'd never return. You might as well have immersed the birds in a bathysphere and introduced them to the orcas, or dosed their food with lysergic acid.

"Let's go," he said, tugging the twins away. Their morsel hands had begun to sweat in his, or he'd begun to sweat onto them. "There's a lot . . . else."

"Orca show!" both girls yelped. It was what they'd come for.

"The show starts at eleven," he told them. "We've got a little time. And there's stuff on the way. Sharks." He'd gathered the implications of the map at a glance: Short of parachuting in, you couldn't get to Shamu Stadium without first passing other enticements. He steered for sharks and giant tortoises, if only as a gambit for skirting the Sesame Street Bay of Play and a roller coaster called Manta.

He had standards. SeaWorld should keep the promise of its name: close encounters with fathoms-deep fauna, not birds, not Elmo, not Princess Leia or Cap'n Crunch. He hardly felt in command of his family's progress here, as they curved on the pathways. He felt squeezed into grooves of expertly predicted responses and behavior, of expenditures of sweat and hilarity and currency from his wallet and also his soul. He was as helpless as a pinball coursing in a tabletop machine. Not one of those simple and friendly, gently decaying machines he'd known in Minneapolis arcades in the seventies, either, but a raging, pulsing nineties-type of pinball machine, half a dozen neon paddles slapping at his brain.

It seemed too much to hope for another Legoland miracle. Two months earlier, Espeseth and his wife and their twin daughters had gone south to visit Legoland. Legoland had been tolerable. Legoland had had variations, textures, edges. It featured some bad zones, including, outstandingly, the bogus municipality called Fun Town, but others were okay, better than okay, like the clutch of restaurants on Castle Hill. There, while the twins got their picture taken with the Queen, and jousted on Lego horses riveted to a train track, he'd been able to sneak off to Castle Ice Cream and obtain a double espresso. That had been something. Hidden with his espresso in a shady quadrant of the castle courtyard, he'd silently toasted his daughters as they'd one after the other rounded the rail. Though he supposed he had Legoland to blame: Its tolerability had led him too easily into agreeing to SeaWorld, which even on Celexa, he now saw, would have been another prospect entirely.

*

His shrink, Irving Renker, had given him a warning about the effects of leaching Celexa from his brain. Espeseth had at the time of the conversation been free of the medicine for just two days. He was quitting under Renker's guidance, such as it was. "Prepare yourself," Renker told him. "You might see bums and pickpockets."

"See in the sense of hallucinate?"

"No," Renker said. "You won't hallucinate. I mean see in the sense of *notice*. You may disproportionately notice bums and pickpockets. Creeps. Perverts. Even amputees."

Irving Renker was a Jewish New Yorker who'd crawled out of his archetype like a lobster from its shell, still conforming to that shell's remorseless shape but wandering around fresh, tender, and amazed. Renker advocated physical exercise and could be seen navigating the crests of Santa Barbara's hills on his bicycle, wearing a helmet and shades as well as an office-ready sweater, blue slacks, and leather-soled shoes. Espeseth had never seen him in the flats, let alone near the beach. He suspected that Renker's wife did all their grocery shopping. Renker's office was in an in-law apartment nestled in the scrubby hills behind his home, itself raised on stilts to meet the angle of the terrain. Renker's front-window drapes were always drawn, thwarting curious eyes. Was there a secret intellectual-

Jew hovel there, with book-lined shelves, Sigmundian fetish masks, funky unfumigatable Persian carpets? No way to know. The consultation room was bland: framed abstract watercolors, beige upholstery, brass clock.

Renker's conversation included, along with the phrases "Keep it simple" and "Don't overthink," terms like "black folks," "Oriental," "gypped," and "bum." Once, as Espeseth reminisced at length about sitting with his three brothers in the front seat of his father's pickup truck on a fishing expedition, Renker had murmured, "Yes, yes, that's known as 'riding Mexican.'"

Espeseth never confronted or corrected his shrink. Instead, he'd gently offer examples of appropriate speech, in this case by replying, "Does this mean that the Celexa was, what, making me blind to homeless people? Or more likely to get robbed?"

"It's a question of emphasis," Renker said. "You may tend to notice scumbags, to the detriment of those standing to the right and the left of them. I don't want to suggest you'll become paranoid, but you may also project scumbaggery onto ordinary people." That his shrink believed in "ordinary people" was a bad sign if Espeseth dwelled on it; he tried not to. It was what Renker said next that he couldn't shake off. "In withdrawal from Celexa some patients have described a kind of atmosphere of rot or corruption or peril creeping around the edges of the everyday world, a thing no one but they can identify. A colleague of mine labeled this 'grub-in-meat syndrome.' Better to be prepared than have it sneak up on you."

Grub-in-meat syndrome?

No one, not shrink Renker, not Espeseth's wife, certainly not the twins, no human listener outside the containment zone of his skull knew that Paul Espeseth had renamed himself Pending Vegan. His secret name was a symptom, if it should be considered a symptom, that had overtaken him months before he quit the Celexa. Could it be a side effect? He'd hoped it would abate when he went off the drug. No such luck. Pending Vegan wasn't completely sorry. His new name was a mortification, yes, but he clung to it, for it also held some promise of an exalted life, one just beyond reach.

How had his researches begun? Espeseth, when that had been his only name, had checked out of Santa Barbara's public library a popular account of the world's collapse into unsustainability under the weight of its human population. He'd gone from that to reading several famous polemics against the cruelty of farms and slaughterhouses. Next, a book called *Fear of the Animal Planet,* which detailed acts of beastly revenge upon human civilization. It was then that Espeseth felt himself becoming Pending Vegan. A knowledge had been born inside him, the development of which only inertia and embarrassment and conformity could slow. Fortunately or unfortunately, Pending Vegan was rich in these delaying properties.

The great obstacle would be in explaining his decision to his daughters. Pending Vegan admired Chloe's and Deirdre's negotiation between their native animal-love and the pleasures of meat-eating. It struck him as a hard-won sophistication, something like F. Scott Fitzgerald's capacity to keep two opposed ideas in mind at the same time. The girls' early rites of passage seemed to consist mainly of such paradox-absorbing efforts. That, for instance, Mommy and Daddy fought but loved each other. That human beings were miraculous and shyness ought to be overcome, yet also that they should violently distrust the too-eager stranger as a probable monster. That an hour of television or the iPad should be judged an intoxicating surfeit, while parents binged on screens at every opportunity. Pending Vegan routinely spent three hours sitting on the couch, watching his football team lose. The Vikings, talisman of his ancestral roots. Yet, unlike the Redskins and the Chiefs, they never had their name and logo criticized as racist. No one felt sorry for white people, which might explain his fascination with Jews, who seemed to have it both ways. Had Irving Renker been eavesdropping on Pending Vegan's thoughts, he would have chortled. *Quit drifting.*

Civilizing children was pretty much all about inducing cognitive dissonance. His daughters' balancing of their desire both to cuddle and to devour mammals was their ticket for entry to the human pageant. If Pending Vegan admitted to them that he now believed it wrong to eat animals—even while he still craved the tang of smoky steaks and salt-greasy bacon—he'd lower himself, in their eyes, to a state of childlike moral absolutism. Or perhaps it would be in his own eyes? He'd been Pending now for six months. Some otherworldly future inquisitor, most likely a pearly-gates sentinel with the head of a piglet or a calf, would hold him accountable for this delay, a thing comparable to the period when the Allies had learned of the existence of the death camps yet checked their moral outrage against military-tactical considerations. Nothing had changed in his eating habits or other behaviors. He hadn't distributed pamphlets or obtained a bumper sticker. Nothing had changed, except that he had awarded himself a secret name.

Boiling in shame, he led his family into the shark-observation area, trudging onto a moving walkway behind other families and their strollers. Another piece of coercive architecture, the passage tunneled beneath the sharks' tanks, illuminating the creatures from below, the better to consider their white bellies and jack-o'-lantern grimaces. It struck him now that the park's design was somehow alimentary. You were being engulfed, digested, shit out.

"I'm scared," Deirdre said.

"But I'm not," Chloe said.

Pending Vegan didn't presume to speak for the sharks. He pointed instead at the glimmer ahead, as the moving walkway ground them out of the darkness.

"Daddy?" Chloe said.

"Yes?"

"Are dolphins and killer whales really people's pets that went back into the sea?"

"Not pets," Pending Vegan said. "Wild animals. Like pigs." He shuddered at the proliferating confusion: The girls knew pigs as farm animals. Just that morning he'd been surreptitiously reading a blog named *The Call of the Feral*. The castes of the subjugated: Pet, Domesticated, Feral, Wild . . .

"Why can't we have a pet?" Chloe asked.

Pending Vegan's wife turned to him. He avoided her eyes, but felt them anyway.

"Your father doesn't like pets," his wife said.

"Almost time for the eleven o'clock show!" he said, desperate to change the subject. And so they slugged out of the shark gallery's gullet into daylight.

All of SeaWorld was squirming.

Grub-in-meat syndrome, the suggestion that Renker had unhelpfully planted, was itself a grub squirming in the meat of Pending Vegan's mind.

*

They'd had a Jack Russell terrier, a neutered two-year-old male named Maurice that they'd adopted from a shelter, a total freaking maniac whom his wife had adored and he—well, Pending Vegan had also adored the dog, though it had been like living with a puzzle he couldn't solve. Maurice moved at bewildering speeds, leaped vertically like an illegal firework, demanded everything, and invaded all their most intimate spaces. And then—and this, the reason that any mention of pets on the part of the girls chastened him, and the reason that his wife's gaze froze his blood—when Pending Vegan had seen the

dog's behavior around his pregnant wife, he'd banished
Maurice from their lives. The dog had been too attentive,
too obsessed with her pregnancy, curling itself along her
stomach at night as if hatching the twins with its own heat.
Maurice had begun snapping at Pending Vegan when he
approached his own marital bed. In the third trimester,
he'd taken the dog back to the shelter, and though this
was barely forgivable, perhaps not forgivable at all, after
the babies came Maurice was never mentioned again.

The girls had no way of knowing they'd been womb-
cuddled by Maurice, unless their mother one day told
them. Chloe and Deirdre instead stanched their mam-
malian craving with Pixar creatures. Driving here, they'd
been attention-glued to video screens mounted on the
backs of their parents' headrests. This spared them the
sameness of I-5, its repetitious suburban exits, noise-
barrier walls, and dead yellowed hills. Near San Diego, a
road sign showed a silhouette of a fleeing Mexican family, like moose or deer, not to be hit in their illegal flight
across the freeway's five lanes. Pending Vegan felt blessed
to be excused from explaining it.

Family life, a cataclysm of solitudes.

As a boy he'd endured backseat travel without the help
of movies. Instead he'd directed his gaze out the family
station wagon's windows, past a zillion miles of the Chip-
pewa National Forest, the U.P., and southern portions of
Ontario and Manitoba. As a ten-year-old, in his ecology
phase, he'd invented a time-killing game known, like his
new name, only to himself. In this fantasy, Espeseth's par-

ents' car featured a long invisible knife, like the wing of a plane, which could extend or retract from the side of the station wagon according to his mental instructions. He and his parents were only pretending to be nobodies, the sole Protestant family from the suburb nicknamed St. Jewish Park. In truth, they were emissaries from another world, sent to reclaim the landscape from the intrusions of the human species. He alone was orchestrating the blade, which shot out to lop off each electrical pole and road sign, and retracted to spare as many trees as possible in the effort. Houses, and other cars, it sliced through mercilessly. His fantasy even included an alibi-providing element of delay, which explained both his not getting to see the glorious destruction he'd wreaked and why no human authority was able to locate and neutralize the mysterious force that tore through his surroundings: The sliced objects fell apart five minutes after his family's car passed by. By this method, the earth would be returned to the flora and fauna.

Lately the image of the invisible blade had returned to Pending Vegan. It would come at the sight of some architectural abomination, or a roadside blighted with billboards. SeaWorld, however, was impervious to the fantasy. Had he begun slicing up this labyrinth of discord, he'd merely murder the creatures trapped within it. By the logic of his childhood fantasy the blade would free the tortoises and the sharks and the porpoises from their tanks, to pour out and die gasping in sunlight on the concrete walkways.

Once inside Shamu Stadium, contra Renker, Pending Vegan noticed no bums and pickpockets. In Shamu Stadium he noticed furloughed military. The soldiers between rotations, out for a day trip with their families, their unfamiliar young children and stoical neglected wives, to see the killer whales. They were knowable by their short haircuts and bicep tattoos, by the wary swivel of their thickened necks. In their upright stolidity it was as though various civilian bodies had all been poured into the same unforgiving mold. Ethnicities reduced to traces in the soldiers were more tangible in the wives and children—in Renkerian terms, mostly black folks, Mexicans, and Orientals. Maybe even a scattering of Gypsies? How to know? *Simplify, simplify.*

Perhaps it was the servicemen who would provide the calamity that Pending Vegan's nervous system shrieked for. He envisioned helicopter footage, yellow tape, SWAT teams milling beside inconsolable families. The stadium was a Mayan temple, one waiting for some sacrifice in the blue pool below. Yet trapped here with five thousand others, Pending Vegan felt for the moment stilled in his crisis. If his voyage through SeaWorld's tubes and tunnels was a sort of peristalsis, he'd reached its multichambered stomach.

And, after the insipid triumphalist overture of music and video and prancing androgynous spandex, when the orcas finally entered the arena and began their leaping, SeaWorld was overwritten by their absolute and devastating presence. By their act of stitching two realms together, sky and water, merely for the delight of a stadium full of children—children who, in response, leaped, too, and vibrated in their seats, and gurgled incoherently, practically speaking in tongues. Other kids, older and more intrepid than his own, raced down to the plastic barrier to be splashed, to stand with their arms flapping. The killer whales, with their Emmett Kelly eyes, were God's glorious lethal clowns. Their plush muscular bodies were the most unashamed things Pending Vegan had ever seen. Like panda bears redesigned by Albert Speer. *Always with the Holocaust references,* Renker once said. *Why don't you leave that to us?*

The twins sat between him and his wife, holding hands, their eyes wide, their incorruptible appetites overwhelmed.

"Deirdre's scared," Chloe said.

"No, I'm not," Deirdre said. She spoke dreamily, not taking her eyes from the pool. Pending Vegan ached to enclose the girls in some kind of protective partition extending from his damaged soul. But the girls were not enclosable, as the stadium was not enclosable, as the world was not. They were all open to the sky, to whatever rays leaked down through the flayed atmosphere. The girls were open to the sky and to killer whales leaping through their undefended hearts. And, anyhow, Pending Vegan had no protective partition extending from his soul. Such a thing was as imaginary as the retractable blade extending from his parents' station wagon.

What would the killer whales mean to the girls when

they eventually learned the facts of the case? The injuries of the world stacked up everywhere, patiently waiting for his daughters' attention. One day they'd find all the documentaries and Web sites on their own. *You may be prone to notice your children,* Renker should have warned him.

Meanwhile, on the other side of the twins, a mystery: Pending Vegan's wife. She with whom he'd once practically merged. Then, as if he'd bumped into her and knocked off two pieces, the twins had appeared. In the past year, she'd become opaque, as though deliberately to spare him. Her human outline now contained what Pending Vegan had named, in conversation with Renker, "the Cloud of Unknowing." She'd ushered him into the Celexa odyssey and abided with him through it, but what now? Was her long-deferred judgment about to fall?

Emerging from Shamu Stadium, Pending Vegan felt he could withstand his wife's judgment, as he could withstand SeaWorld, as SeaWorld could withstand itself. Neither the veterans nor the orcas nor he had wigged out and chomped or bayoneted anyone. If the orca show was the climax, the test, oughtn't they depart? He yearned for the petty solaces of the motel, his family sorted onto twin doubles, with room-service club sandwiches, more pay-per-view Disney.

"So," he said, clapping his hands together. "Find the parking lot?"

"These are all-day tickets," his wife said. "Rebecca's mom told us not to miss out on the pet show."

"I'm hungry," he said.

"The pet show, the pet show!" the girls chanted.

"There's food here," his wife said crisply. "And we drove here and paid for all-day entry. The girls have waited months." This time Pending Vegan's wife found his eyes before he could avert, and he was enveloped in the Cloud of Unknowing.

*

The next pet show began at one, so they parked their stroller in a shady spot and Pending Vegan went looking for something edible. He found a pizzeria, but the wait for a table was impossible, and he couldn't imagine pushing into its dark interior even to order something to take away. Outside the restaurant, however, a man grilled turkey legs at a stand. The drumsticks looked oddly primal—this wasn't Medieval Times, after all!—but the odor of the seared meat set Pending Vegan to slavering.

See food, eat food.

Sea World, Eat World.

The instant he made the purchase he regretted it. The drumsticks were meat waste, discarded by some factory farm in preference for the breast product. SeaWorld might as well be selling horse hooves or pickled cow eyeballs. Still, he walked it back to the stroller, feeling like Fred Flintstone. Under his wife's incredulous gaze he tore shreds off the huge cartilaginous drumstick to feed to the girls, like a mother bird to nested fledglings. The crackling greasy skin came off whole and, once removed, was too revolting to do anything with other than discard. The girls washed the meat down with orange juice. Paper napkins stuck and tore on their faces and fingers.

With fifteen minutes still to spare, they diverted to the bat-ray petting tank. As with the flamingos, Pending Vegan had to jostle the twins to the front for their chance to immerse their hands in the shallow, waist-high tank and let the blunt, rubbery rays slip beneath them. The girls gasped at the sensation. This might be what it would feel like to touch a killer whale. Here might be the true connection at last, the thing they'd really come for, and for a moment again the barriers all vanished for Pending Vegan, the turkey eyeballs forgotten, the piped-in music turned to something transporting, as if from the distant spheres.

For some reason the tank full of eloquent rays also housed a horny, knuckle-faced sturgeon. A sign warned those petting the rays not to try to touch the sturgeon. Pending Vegan, in his rapture, tried to touch it. The fish's furrowed brow seemed to want his consolation. The sturgeon in response snapped its jaws up at him where he stood amid so many merry children, his own and others. Pending Vegan jerked backward in fear. The sturgeon continued on its course, grub within the meat of the ray tank.

"Did you see that?" he asked his daughters and anyone else who might bear witness.

"See what?" Chloe said.

"The sturgeon! It practically barked at me!"

"Daddy," Chloe said affectionately.

*

The pet show had a stadium of its own, a smaller arena, basically a set of bleachers mounted before a stage featuring ladders, windows, obstacle courses, and giant plastic sculptures of a milk bottle and a bright-red sneaker. Unlike the seats in Shamu Stadium, those here were sparsely filled, and Pending Vegan and his wife and children found places in the third row. After only a moment the show began. In a sort of pre-credit sequence, a stream of dogs and house cats coursed out of various trapdoors over the Astroturf stage, followed by a pig, an ostrich, and a string of ducklings, to the tune of "Who Let the Dogs Out?" The dogs jumped on a seesaw and flipped miniature plastic burgers at a fake stove. The cats climbed a rope. The twins were enthralled. One of the dogs pulled a lever to release a rolled-up banner that read, in nails-on-chalkboard font, the show's title: PETS RULE!

"That's a classic example of Hitler's Big Lie technique right there, wouldn't you say?" Pending Vegan said.

"What is?" his wife said.

"'Pets Rule!' They don't. They just . . . don't. I hate it here."

"Sh-h-h."

"We're complicit with a well-recognized nightmare."

"I've never seen any criticism of the pet show."

That's because everyone's too busy scrubbing their brains of aesthetic and moral calamity, he wished to say. *After such knowledge, what forgiveness?* Instead he said, "That sturgeon back there almost took my finger off."

"Too late, I think."

"What, for the fish to eat my finger?"

"No, I mean too late for you and the fish to get on *60 Minutes,* since this place already had its media moment."

An emcee in a baseball costume and a headset microphone emerged and began introducing the pet show. Some failed actor, Pending Vegan supposed. His head shot having landed on SeaWorld's human-resources desk, the kid was fated to deliver this obnoxious script five times daily. He described the Pet Olympics, in which the trained dogs would compete, then gave the star performers' names as each appeared, beckoning to the children in the crowd to clap and squeal at each shameless antic. "All our dogs are rescue animals," he explained. "They train for up to three years before making their debut in 'Pets Rule!,' and you're very lucky, because we have a 'Pets Rule!' rookie debuting today, a great little guy named Bingo. When I bring him on I want you to appreciate that he's going in front of a crowd for the first time, so I hope you'll give Bingo your love, give him your warmest reception—"

Bingo was a Jack Russell terrier. He seemed, at first, ready for prime time, flipping over twice, then operating with his jaw a bright-red wrench on an outsized fire hydrant, resulting in a burst of water that sprayed over a bystander piglet and into the faces of the first-row spectators, who screamed in pleasure. He stood on his hind legs, grinning widely, to gobble a discreet reward from the palm of the emcee. Then the new dog bounded from the stage, scrambled over the first two rows of seats, and into Pending Vegan's arms. There Bingo begin frantically licking and nibbling Pending Vegan's chin and lips, with tiny sharp nips mixed in behind the swirling tongue.

"Bingo!" the emcee called from the stage. The wet piglet wandered off erratically, but chortling music continued to pour from the speakers, lending an atmosphere of hilarity. The dog now applied itself furiously to Pending Vegan's nostrils. Whether this was part of the show or not Pending Vegan was undecided. Chloe and Deirdre responded with delight, reaching to fondle the dog that pressed their father back in his seat. His wife touched the dog, too, and Pending Vegan felt her arm graze his stomach, the first time in months. Others in their row shrank slightly away.

It was their former animal, rescued once and abandoned, rescued a second time and trained, now restored to them. Bingo was Maurice, Pending Vegan understood. Like him, the dog had two names. It had recognized Pending Vegan immediately and leaped from the stage to apologize for having abandoned their family, the man and the woman and the twin girls who were now on the outside of the wife's body instead of the inside, where Maurice had last known them. The dog had come to honor the alpha in his former pack. With his animal cunning Maurice perceived that Pending Vegan was off the drug now. Unless that was insane. It was insane. The ostrich had ducked from behind a curtain and goose-stepped to the lip of the stage, obviously off cue. The pet show was in tatters. *An ostrich was not a pet.* Pending Vegan's crimes had a life of their own, yet the dog would, in its automatic way, offer absolution, especially given hands smeared with turkey juice. Pending Vegan's crimes screamed to the infinite horizon. *Quit globalizing,* said the Irving Renker in Pending Vegan's head, as the terrier's frantic tongue drilled into the webbing between his fingers.

AS SHE CLIMBED ACROSS THE TABLE

Philip is in love with Alice. As the novel opens, he is beginning to lose her. Not to another man, as he fears, but to, quite literally, nothing. Alice is a physicist, and a team at the university, where both she and Philip work, has created a hole, a doorway of nothingness inside the laboratory. They call it Lack, and Alice becomes obsessed with it, just as Philip is obsessed with her. *As She Climbed Across the Table* is an astute and wise portrait of unrequited love (albeit of a very unusual kind), a hilarious academic parody, a novel of ideas, and a social satire. Though utterly original, it finds itself in the school of Thomas Pynchon, Don DeLillo, Katherine Dunn, and David Foster Wallace.

Fiction

CHRONIC CITY

Chase Insteadman, former child television star, has a new role in life—permanent guest on the Upper East Side dinner party circuit, where he is consigned to talk about his astronaut fiancée, Janice Trumbull, who is trapped on a circling space station. A chance encounter collides Chase with Perkus Tooth, a wily pop culture guru with a vicious conspiratorial streak and the best marijuana in town. Despite their disparate backgrounds and trajectories, Chase and Perkus discover they have a lot in common, including a cast of friends from all walks of life in Manhattan. Together and separately they attempt to define the indefinable, and enter into a quest for the most elusive of things: truth and authenticity in a city where everything has a price.

Fiction

In a volume he describes as "a series of covert and not-so-covert autobiographical pieces," Jonathan Lethem explores the nature of cultural obsession—from western films and comic books to the music of Pink Floyd and the New York City subway. Along the way, he shows how each of these "voyages out from himself" has led him to the source of his beginnings as a writer. *The Disappointment Artist* is a series of windows onto the collisions of art, landscape, and personal history that formed Lethem's richly imaginative, searingly honest perspective on life. A touching, deeply perceptive portrait of a writer in the making.

Essays/Criticism

ALSO AVAILABLE

Dissident Gardens
The Esctasy of Influence
The Fortress of Solitude
Girl in Landscape
Men and Cartoons
Motherless Brooklyn
You Don't Love Me Yet

VINTAGE CONTEMPORARIES
Available wherever books are sold.
www.vintagebooks.com